jumping off swings

jumping
off
swings

Jo Knowles

Copyright © 2009 by Johanna Knowles

First edition 2009

Library of Congress Cataloging-in-Publication Data
Knowles, Johanna (Johanna Beth), date.
Jumping off swings / Jo Knowles. —1st ed.
p. cm.
Summary: Tells, from four points of view, the ramifications of a pregnancy
resulting from a "one-time thing" between Ellie, who feels loved when boys
touch her, and Josh, an eager virgin with a troubled home life.
ISBN 978-0-7636-3949-5
[1. Sex—Fiction. 2. Pregnancy—Fiction. 3. Interpersonal relations—
Fiction. 4. Emotional problems—Fiction.] I. Title.
PZ7.K7621Jum 2009
[Fic]—dc22   2009004587

2 4 6 8 10 9 7 5 3 1

For Debbi Michiko Florence and Cindy Faughnan —
writing partners, friends, sisters.
In our next lives, I hope we go to the same high school.

part one

SEPTEMBER

chapter 1

Ellie

I CAN STILL FEEL A TRACE of his warm lips against mine as he slips away from me and fumbles for the door to his father's van. I stay lying under the scratchy wool blanket on the backseat, wishing he'd stay. When he slides the door open, the ceiling light blinks on and exposes our faces to each other. His hair is rumpled. His brown eyes avoid mine.

"Thanks, Ellie. See you inside?"

I nod.

He slides the door shut and leaves me in the dark.

Thanks, Ellie.

I sit up and reach under my shirt to reclasp my bra as his shadow makes its way across the lawn and back to the house. He doesn't turn around.

I find my own way to the door handle and slide the heavy door open again. When the light comes on, I see the crumpled-up wool blanket on the backseat. It's covered with dog hair, and so is my shirt. I try to brush off the hairs, but they cling to the cotton. I climb out and adjust my clothes in the light, then slide the door shut. I lean against the cool metal and breathe in the clean night air.

Up at the house, indoor lights make the rooms look like they're glowing. Party noises echo across the lawn. Through the large picture window in the living room, I see him standing with a group of guys. Someone hands him a beer. They throw their heads back, laughing. He joins them. Someone grabs his hand and smells it. He pulls his hand back, but the others try to grab and smell it, too.

I squeeze my legs together.

He pushes his friends away and walks to the window. His face is suddenly serious, looking out at the dark, not seeing me.

I slide my body along the side of the van and hide behind it just in case.

"Ellie?" Corinne's footsteps hurry down the driveway. "Ellie?" she calls again.

"Over here," I say quietly.

"There you are! I was worried when you didn't come in with — Ellie? Are you OK?"

"I don't feel so well," I say, making my way to a nearby tree.

She follows. "Do you need to get sick?"

"I think so —" I am already bending over, retching.

Corinne instinctively pulls my hair back.

I retch and retch, but nothing comes out.

When I finally stop, Corinne helps me fix my hair and we find her car.

"You are the only person I know who can throw up without throwing anything up," she says as she starts the engine. "Jeez. How many drinks did you have, anyway?"

I shrug.

None.

"I keep telling you you've got to pace yourself."

"I know," I say quietly.

We drive a minute in silence.

"So . . ." She taps her fingers on the steering wheel. "How was it?"

I feel his hand in mine, leading me outside. See his brown eyes staring back at me, then closing as he leans in to kiss me.

"OK."

"Just OK? But Josh is so cute! I nearly died of jealousy when I saw you disappearing with him. Come on, give me some juice."

I feel his warm, wet whisper in my ear.

Ellie. Oh, Ellie.

"It was nice at first."

I lick my lips, remembering how his mouth felt pressed against mine. How his hands rubbed my back.

Your skin is so soft.

My stomach melted at his touch.

"So what happened?"

Let me touch you.

I feel his fingers reaching under my panties and pressing inside me.

"I don't want to talk about it."

"Come on! Far? Farther? Or farthest?" She's smiling as she concentrates on the road.

Thanks, Ellie.

I cross my legs.

"That's between me and him," I say.

"You never tell me anything! It's not fair."

I look out the window and watch the dark trees on the side of the road. My reflection in the glass stares back at me.

"Are you going to see him again?"

I turn away from my reflection and concentrate on the yellow lines disappearing into the blackness in front of us.

"No," I say. "It was just a one-time thing."

chapter 2

Caleb

"SO, WAS SHE TOTALLY INTO IT?" Kyle asks.

"What do you think?" Josh smirks at us as if his new status has elevated him from virgin geek to ultrastud.

My best friend has officially become an asshole.

"Dude, way to hook up on the first try!" Dave high-fives Josh, then gives me a sympathetic look, like "Too bad you're still a loser, buddy."

My second best friend has officially joined my best friend in the Asshole Club.

My hands close into fists. If they weren't talking about Ellie, maybe I wouldn't mind so much. Maybe that makes me an asshole, too.

"Easy come, easy go," Josh says.

Dave laughs and elbows Josh. "Cum. Get it?"

They both crack up. Some other guys start to laugh, too.

The locker room is steamy from the showers and smells like a battle is going on between sweat, smelly feet, and wet soap. The soap is losing. I feel like I'm trapped in a lame locker room scene in some made-for-TV movie where all the guys are a bunch of stereotypical pricks.

"Told ya she was a sure thing," Ben says as he sprays a cloud of deodorant under his arms.

"Yup, all you have to do is get her alone." Kyle grins and closes his eyes, as if he's remembering.

"Now we just have to find someone for Special Cay, here," Dave says, like he's so experienced. "Maybe you could hook up with her at the next party. She's obviously not picky if she'd do it with these losers."

They all laugh, even though the joke is about them. And Ellie. God, I can't believe it. Ellie was with Ben? And Kyle? And *Josh*? I imagine how good it would feel to beat the crap out of all of them, but I'm obviously outnumbered. Some of them probably have more muscle in one arm than I have in my entire body.

"No, thanks," I kind of mumble. I start shoving my stuff in my bag.

Dave shrugs and throws his backpack over his shoulder. "See you girls later."

"Hey, wait up. Can you drop me off?" Josh grabs his bag. He struts after Dave in his new I'm-not-a-virgin-anymore walk.

The rest of the guys follow, leaving me alone in their stench.

I've had a crush on Ellie since first grade, when she gave me her red toy Porsche. The doors opened, and you could move the seats back and forth. I still have it on the top shelf of my bookcase behind the set of Narnia books my dad sent me for my sixth birthday. In the card, he promised we'd have a long visit some summer and he'd read the whole series to me. Four years later, I gave up waiting and read them myself.

I shake my head and pick up my bag. I should have known I had about as much of a chance with Ellie as I had of my dad actually fulfilling one of his promises. Why would she pick the pasty, scrawny guy who trips at the sight of her when she could have . . . anyone else?

chapter 3

Corinne

"I thought he was different," Ellie says quietly.

I have to lie down on my bed for this phone conversation. Judging from how it's going so far, it'll be hard not to suffocate myself with my pillow. Not to be insensitive, but this is like the fourth time this has happened, and it's getting old. I should have known it would turn out like this. It always does. Ellie acts like hooking up is no big deal, then a few days later calls me in tears.

"How would you know if he was different?" I ask. "You hooked up with him as soon as he smiled at you."

"That's not what happened!"

"Then how *did* it happen?"

I want to tell her that from my point of view, it seems like all a guy has to do is give her a compliment and she'll disappear with him to some back room.

But she's really crying now.

"El, I'm sorry. I'm just trying to help you. You keep getting hurt."

"He was so sweet to me at the party. He held my hand and acted like we were a couple! I thought maybe he really wanted more than just sex."

"Then why didn't you stop him when things started going too far?"

"Because I didn't realize until after he left me!"

"Ellie! You could have *asked* first. That's how it works!"

"How would *you* know?"

Right. She has me there. I'm not exactly the authority on sex. Not that she's been any help in that department. I mean if *I* had sex, I'm sure I'd tell Ellie every detail. And to be honest? I had expected the same from her, which was a huge disappointment. But I've heard enough through my sister's bedroom wall when my parents aren't home to know that sex *can* involve talking. Ava's number-one rule: "If you're gonna be with a guy, you need to make sure right off the bat that *you* are the one calling the shots. You say what you want and what you don't want. Period." She's been with her boyfriend for two years. She must know what she's talking about because that guy adores her. And like I said, judging from the noises they make, they are *both* having a good time.

But Ellie's not the type of person to ever put herself first. It's just not who she is.

I listen to her quiet crying and try to think of something to say that could possibly help. Poor Ellie has this romantic idea in her head that is just so fairy-tale, despite what keeps happening. It makes me want to cry.

"That bastard. I'm sorry, El. Has he called you?"

"No. He won't."

"Guys are jerks. You can't trust any of them."

"I thought he would be different," Ellie tells me again. "But then he just left me there. He went back inside and—"

"And what?"

She's crying again.

"What did he do?"

"Nothing," she says, all quiet.

I don't know why she gets into these messes. She's supposed to be the innocent one. But look at us. I'm Miss Horny Forever Virgin and Ellie's, well, not.

"Hey," I say. "Want to meet somewhere? We could go to the mall or something."

"The park?"

"I'll meet you there in twenty minutes," I tell her. "At the swings. And Ellie? Cheer up. It's his loss. I mean it."

I hang up and grab a wrinkled sweatshirt from the end of my bed. I put on my baseball hat and pull it down low. When I check myself in the mirror, I notice the strip of black-and-white photos Ellie and I took in a photo booth at the beginning of the summer. I'm sticking out my tongue and crossing my eyes. Ellie's laughing because she can't manage to cross her own eyes without putting her finger in front of her nose. We laughed so hard that day. School had just gotten out, and we'd gone to the beach to celebrate our freedom. We hung out at the arcade and ate French fries and bought cheap matching earrings from a vendor on the boardwalk.

I step closer and look again at our happy faces. I'd give anything for us to feel like that again.

chapter 4

Josh

"HAND ME THAT WRENCH, BUD."

My dad's huge callused hand reaches out from under the hood of his van. The lines in his palm are black with grease.

"I wonder if the rings are burned out. Didn't I just change the oil two weeks ago?"

I shrug, then remember he can't see me.

"Why don't you make yourself useful and pull out the backseat for me. I told Mikey I'd pick up the speakers for the show tonight."

I roll my eyes and head for the back of the van. My dad playing at the local Legion Club with a bunch of his old high-school buddies doesn't actually count as a "show" in my book, but whatever.

I open the back of the van and reach for the locks to unhitch the backseat. When I tip the seat back to pull it out, Rosie's rumpled blanket slides across my arms.

I swear I smell Ellie's perfume on it.

I cringe at the memory and try to shake it out of my head. I toss the blanket over my shoulder and finish pulling the seat out. As I carry the seat to the back wall of the garage, the blanket slips to the floor. I trip on it and drop the seat.

"Nice play, Shakespeare," my dad says, poking his head out from under the hood of the van.

My dad the comedian. I lean the seat against the wall, then pick up the blanket. The memory flashes in front of me again. I throw the blanket back in the van and slam the door, but it's too late. I've seen her. The way she looked at me as I left her, as if she wanted something. I don't know what. Or maybe I do. But I was so embarrassed by the whole thing, I just wanted to get the hell out of there.

All the guys said how great it would be. How into it Ellie was. No strings, just a good time. They never mentioned how she'd look after. Maybe they didn't notice.

My dad slams the hood of the van. "Come on, I need a beer."

I follow his hulky body through the garage and into the kitchen. Rosie, our mangy-looking mutt that my dad says is a black Lab, drags her fat body up off the garage floor and follows us.

If my mom was home, no way would Dad be slinging one back yet. Not before five o'clock. That's Mom's rule. But she's at work, as usual. And when there's no Mom, there're no rules.

My dad reaches into the fridge and pulls out two cans, handing one to me.

"To Saturdays," he says, touching his can to mine.

The beer is cold in my hand. I crack it open and take a long swig as my dad tilts his own head back and lets the beer empty down his throat. His Adam's apple bobs up and down as he swallows.

When the phone rings, my dad answers in his friendly manner. "Yeah?" He turns his back to me and looks out the window.

"Mikey! How's it goin'? You ready for the gig tonight? Katie *did* forgive you for getting home so late last time, right?" He pauses and takes another swig while he listens to Mike — that's his best friend, and Dave's dad. They've known each other since grade school, just like me and Dave. Our moms, too.

This is the usual routine. Our dads call each other the morning of "the show" and reminisce about last week's performance. Then they talk about their "playlist" like they are a real band and like the list actually changes from week to week. Then they complain about our moms and how they give them such a hard time about staying out too late and drinking too much.

"Well, you'll just have to put your foot down!" my dad says.

Clearly, Dave's mom hasn't quite forgiven his dad yet. I have to laugh at my dad's advice. Like *he* ever stands up to my mom. Actually, they pretty much just ignore each other.

I take another long drink of my beer while my dad does his usual ramble with Mike. He laughs about something Mike says, then swigs. When he finishes his beer, he tosses the can in the sink and opens the fridge for another. I finish my own and drop it in the sink so it hits his.

"Where you going?" he asks me, cupping the mouthpiece on the phone with his hand.

I shrug and head for the door.

"Be good!" he calls after me. I turn around to fire a comeback, but he waves me away and goes back to talking with Mike.

It's warm and sunny outside. The leaves are starting to change color. It smells like fall, and for some reason it reminds me of the day I learned to ride my bike. My dad was sleeping one off, and my mom was determined to teach me on her own — Dad's punishment for getting wasted again.

I was happy to have her to myself, even though he was the one who had promised to teach me.

"You can do it, Joshy, if you just try," she kept saying. She hung on to the back of the seat and wouldn't let me fall. It must have been three hours, maybe longer, till I finally went forward without her. I wobbled all the way to the end of the driveway, then slowly turned back toward her outstretched arms. Her face was all sweaty, and her hair was falling out of her ponytail. She had a huge grin on her face. I swear that's the last time I saw her look genuinely happy.

Now I'm lucky to see her at all. She practically lives at the nursing home, changing old people's diapers and putting their teeth in. Like that is preferable to being at her real home with us. If she's not at work, she's doing some volunteer project with Dave's mom. She used to make my dad and me go with her to the local soup kitchen every Sunday afternoon, but eventually she got tired of us complaining. Plus I think she was embarrassed to bring my dad, who was usually hungover.

I walk to the end of the driveway and look back at the house. The blue vinyl siding is faded and cracked, and the white gutters are overflowing with muck. A few years ago, my mom would have flipped over that. Now nothing around here seems to matter to her. Including us.

I head down the street toward Dave's house. Judging from my dad's side of the phone conversation, Dave'll be wanting to get as far away from his parents as possible. When they fight, it's not pretty. But at least they still acknowledge each other's existence.

I take a left onto Dave's street and look down toward the end, where his house is. Figures. He's already walking toward me.

chapter 5
Ellie

THE METAL CHAINS above me creak as I swing.

Back and forth.

Back and forth.

I pump my legs like I did in first grade. My stomach does a familiar hop each time I swing backward.

When I see Corinne coming toward me, I stop pumping. When she reaches me, she stands so close I almost kick her ⸺ with my feet. She doesn't say anything, just nods hello. She gets on the swing next to me and swings sideways so we almost collide. We used to call it bumper cars when we were little. Only then we used to smash into each other. This time she seems careful not to touch me.

"I'm sorry it didn't work out with Josh." She sees me notice the pity in her eyes and turns away. She starts to swing the right way. She smiles at the breeze and then at me.

I start to pump again, until we are in perfect rhythm. Higher and higher. Our feet point toward the sky.

"Remember how we used to think we could swing right up over the bar?" Corinne asks. "I always thought I could do it if I just pumped hard enough."

We both laugh a little, remembering. We stop pumping at the same time, letting ourselves glide back and forth together. The wind blows my hair forward, then back. Forward, then back.

Corinne used to jump off the swings when we were kids. Just let go of the chains and take flight without a trace of fear. I'd watch her jump, wishing I could be that brave. But I'd always hang on, waiting to slow down first, always mindful of my mother's warning: *You'll break a leg if you're not careful!* But now I don't care.

I send myself jetting into the air. Corinne shrieks in surprise. I'm flying. Just for a second. But I'm flying.

When I land hard on my feet, the sting goes all the way up to my teeth.

Corinne lands heavily beside me and falls to the ground. I fall down next to her. We laugh out loud and roll around, pretending to be injured. It feels so good. My stomach muscles ache from not being used to laughing.

But then Corinne stops. And I think, Don't stop now. Don't stop. Keep laughing. I don't want this to end.

But she's looking behind me, into the distance. She stops smiling. And I know by the look on her face. I know before I turn around. He's here.

chapter 6

Caleb

"PASS ME THAT PAINTBRUSH next to the blue bottle, would you, hon? I need a rougher bristle."

I find the brush and hand it to my mom.

"Tell me what you learned this week."

I shrug. It's the same thing she's said to me since I was in first grade. It's our Saturday-morning-in-the-studio thing. Shrugging or answering "nothing" is not allowed. She'll wait.

"Josh is an asshole," I finally tell her.

"Hmm." She studies a neat row of three cobalt-blue bottles sitting on a paint-spattered step stool. On her canvas are three sort-of ovals of various shades of blue. They look more like giant lava-lamp blobs than bottles, but my mom isn't the type of artist who paints by numbers.

Finally she looks up at me. "Are you going to tell me why?"

"You don't want to know."

She raises her eyebrows, then turns back to her paints. She knows I'll tell her eventually.

She squeezes some more dark-blue paint out of the tube onto an old, chipped plate. It makes a familiar squirty sound, which she used to say, "Pardon me" after, to make me laugh. She winks at me, but I'm not in the mood.

I pick up another paintbrush and stroke the dry bristles across my hand.

She stops mashing her brush into the paint. "Are you going to tell me what's up, or what?"

I sigh. "Josh lost his virginity."

She puts her hands on her knees. "And?"

It's true. Technically, this would not actually qualify Josh as an asshole.

"It was with someone I know," I say.

She goes back to mixing her blues. "You mean someone you care about. Or—someone *you* wanted to have sex with?"

"No! I mean—maybe. I mean—*no!*"

She waits.

"It was Ellie."

"Oh." My mom knows I've had a crush on Ellie since I knew what one was. "Did Josh know about your feelings for her?"

"I dunno. Maybe."

"Did you ever tell him?"

"Not exactly."

"And he's still an asshole?"

"If you heard him talk about her, yeah! They were talking about Ellie like she'll hook up with *anyone*. I thought Ellie was different. I really thought she was special."

My mom adds more dark blue to a bottle. "So tell me." She dabs at the canvas with hard strokes that make the easel shake. "Since when does having sex make someone less special?"

"It's not that. It's just—I never thought Josh would be the type to brag about who he's been with. And I never thought Ellie would be the type to—you know—hook up with so many people."

She adds black to the bottle, turning its insides midnight blue. "Maybe there's a reason for what she's doing."

"You'd have to have a pretty messed-up reason to hook up with those losers, if you ask me."

She shrugs. "What about Josh?"

"What about him?"

"What do you think his reason was?"

"To get laid so the guys will get off his back?"

"You really believe that?"

"I don't know anymore. Maybe? Josh used to tell me he wouldn't do it with just anyone. But he'd never say that in front of the guys. It's like, when the two of us hang out alone, he's different. He's not all, 'Look at me. I'm such a stud.' He's cool. Same with Dave, mostly. But at school they both totally change."

She steps back from her work and studies my face. "Think about what you just said."

"What?"

"When they're with you, they're different."

"And?"

"It's *you*. You help them be themselves when the three of you are together. Not everyone can do that."

"Yeah, right."

"I am right. You don't give yourself enough credit."

I sink back into my chair and watch her paint. She pushes the brush against the blue, making it darker and darker.

I would like to believe that Josh wouldn't have hooked up with Ellie if he knew about my thing for her, but I don't know. Maybe it's my fault for not trusting him enough to tell him in the first place. Maybe I don't give *him* enough credit, either.

chapter 7

Josh

"Oh, shit. Let's get outta here," I say. But Dave is already charging ahead.

Ellie's sitting on the ground next to Corinne. For some reason, they're covered in dry grass. Corinne gives me the evil eye while Ellie turns away. I try to grab Dave's arm and steer him in the other direction, but he takes a step forward out of my reach.

"Going for a roll in the hay?" Dave asks them, like he's suddenly the wittiest bastard around.

"Ha, ha," Corinne says, brushing the brown grass off of her. "Would that turn you on?"

Dave smirks and gives Ellie this "I know what you did" look, but she doesn't see because she's still looking away from us.

"Would you *like* it if it turned me on?" Dave asks.

Corinne rolls her eyes. "Uh—no?" She stands up and brushes the grass off her jeans, then nudges Ellie with her knee to get up, too.

Ellie pushes herself up but doesn't bother to brush herself off. She fixes her eyes on the ground, her feet, anywhere but on us.

Dave elbows me and gestures for me to say something to her.

"Um, great party the other night," I say.

Dave gives an amused grunt. Corinne glares at me. She looks like she wants to kill me as badly as I want to kill Dave.

"Um, I mean—" I start to say.

Ellie finally looks up and meets my eyes for a split second. I recognize something there, but I'm not sure what. All I know is that look makes me feel like crap.

Corinne takes hold of Ellie's arm, and they head for the parking lot without saying a word. As they leave, Corinne shakes her head at us, as if to say, "See ya, assholes."

"Those two need to lighten up," Dave says.

I'm sure they can hear him, but they don't turn around.

Dave. God, he's so clueless that you can't help but feel sorry for him.

"Women," I say, like I'm joking. But I see Ellie's face in the light of the van. And I see me, just leaving her there.

Dave elbows me under the ribs. "Look at you, Mr. Heartbreaker." He cracks up.

I fight the urge to beat the shit out of him.

"Let's just get out of here." I start walking back the way we came. Fast. Dave practically has to jog to keep up.

"What's your problem?" he asks, finally getting that this isn't a joke. "You gonna let them own the park? They don't own the fucking park! This is *our* place."

"Shut up," I say. It's like I'm talking to a five-year-old.

"What the hell?"

"Just shut up. Seriously."

Dave follows me out of the park. We walk for a while down the streets of our neighborhood. But there's nowhere to go, so we end up back at my house.

As soon as I open the door, Rosie runs over to us, her nails clicking on the wood floor. I call out to my dad but he doesn't answer, and when we walk by the couch in the living room, we see him sacked out on the sofa. His shirt is all grimy from working on the van. It stretches out around his gut, making it look like a big, smooth stone. A Budweiser sits on his guitar case next to the couch. He doesn't like to practice when I'm home. He used to play in front of me when I was little, even sang to me, but not anymore.

Dave snickers as we sneak past him and into the kitchen. I want to punch him because I don't think it's funny and probably his dad is doing the same thing at their house. Instead, I take two beers out of a Bud Suitcase and toss one to Dave. He catches the can and smiles like he's a freakin' dog getting a treat. I pat him on the head as a joke, but he just looks confused. We head to my room.

"What's Ellie's problem, anyway?" Dave asks me after we've had a few swigs. "I thought you two hooked up? Something go wrong?" He's sitting on my bed with his legs stretched out, crossed at his feet. I want to tell him to get his smelly shoes off my bed, but I don't have the energy.

"I don't know," I say. "It wasn't exactly, you know, like the guys said it would be."

"What do you mean?" He actually looks concerned, which is kind of surprising for Dave.

"It was—just forget it. It doesn't matter. It's over. Who cares?"

He shrugs. "I'll drink to that," he says, and downs the rest of his beer.

So much for his concern.

I chug the rest of my beer, too.

I sit on the floor and lean back against the wall. When I close my eyes, I feel her all over again. Her skin was warm, like a flannel shirt. Her hair smelled clean and sweet. Her arms around me, holding me, made me feel real. I had no idea what I was doing, but it felt so good.

Then it was over — way too fast. Like, embarrassingly fast. I knew I shouldn't have taken off right after, but I felt like such an idiot.

I open my eyes and catch Dave squeezing a zit. "Stubborn fucker," he says.

I shake my head to let him know I think he's a pig and close my eyes again. But as soon as I do, I see her face. The way she looked at me when I left her. Like she knew I wasn't just going back to the party. Like I was deserting her.

And that's when I realize why that look is familiar. I've seen it before. On my mom's face. It's the look she used to carry around every Sunday morning when my dad started coming home later and later from his "shows" with Mikey. She'd say how she'd been waiting up for him, worried, and he'd get all mad at her. Like how dare *she* be mad at *him* for having a little fun after working his ass off all week? How the shows were paid gigs and why shouldn't he be able to relax with a few drinks afterward? He really knew how to turn things around.

My mom would look at him with this questioning expression like, *What happened to you?* And that would piss him off more. Then she'd tell me to go outside. I'd sit on the concrete step by the front door and listen.

Why are you doing this to yourself?

I'm not doing anything. Just having a little fun after a long week.

What kind of message do you think you're giving Josh?

What the hell are you talking about?

You have a problem.

Yeah, a nagging wife who doesn't appreciate me or my music.

It was always the same. My mom would end up crying, and my dad would go into their bedroom and slam the door.

I'd take off and meet up with Dave, whose own parents no doubt had sent him out of the house, too. We'd wander around, like today, always ending up at the park. We thought of it as *our* park.

Sometimes we'd catch Caleb there, too. The first time we saw him, we must have been about eight, and definitely the only kids our age at the park without some adoring parent telling us some bullshit about how good we were at throwing a ball or running or whatever. Whenever the three of us needed someplace to go, we went to the park.

But not now. Not if I might run into Ellie.

The guys were full of shit. There were plenty of strings attached; they just didn't stick around to see them. And, asshole that I am, I saw them and didn't stick around, either.

chapter 8

Corinne

AFTER I WALK ELLIE TO HER HOUSE, we go to her room and hang out. Every time I try to get her to talk about Josh, she shakes her head and changes the music on her stereo. After a while, her mom calls us downstairs for an early dinner. We sit at the kitchen table while her mom heats up macaroni and cheese— the real kind with cracker crumbs on the top and everything.

"Thanks. This looks delicious!" I say when she puts a heaping plate in front of me.

She smiles and puts a matching plate next to Ellie. Ellie's mom isn't a big talker. She's more like a server. It's kind of weird. Also, I've always had the impression that she doesn't like me very much. Probably because of my sister's "reputation." News of the abortion she had last year spread around town, and I guess people think that kind of thing runs in families. Jeez, I can only imagine how much she'd freak if Ellie's mom knew the real deal about her own daughter. The woman prides herself on perfection, and not just her own.

"Let me know if you need anything else," she says.

Ellie nods. "Thanks, Mom."

We wait for her to leave before we start eating. The noodles are surprisingly tasteless. I think she must have used fat-free cheese and definitely no salt. I search the table for a saltshaker but don't see one. Ellie moves her food around but doesn't even bother to take a taste. I force down a few more bites and then give up.

"OK," I finally say. "I'm not leaving until we talk this out."

"Shhh," Ellie says, actually putting her finger to her lips.

I look around in an exaggerated way to remind her we're alone.

"Ellie, I'm serious," I whisper. "Why do you keep doing this? Every time you hook up with someone, you get totally depressed after. It makes no sense."

She's quiet a minute, then puts down her fork.

"I don't know."

"Well—you need to stop. I mean, God, Ellie. I don't want to make you feel bad or anything, but how many guys have you been with now?"

She covers her face with her hands and shakes her head. A sob escapes through her fingers.

Crap.

"I'm sorry, El. Seriously. It's not your fault. I don't know why these guys use you, OK? Maybe it's because they know you're too nice to stop them. But Ellie, just because a guy is nice to you doesn't mean you owe him anything."

She drags her fingers down her cheeks as if she'd like to scratch them.

"You don't understand what it's like. How it feels."

"Try me."

She studies her plate as if she's looking for an answer, but she doesn't say anything. We sit there for what seems like forever.

Finally, she takes a deep breath and says very quietly, "I can't. I can't explain. I just . . . when I'm with them, I feel . . . like they care about me. I feel special. I feel like they *want* me. Not just my body but *me*. Like they could *love* me. But . . . I'm always wrong. No one wants me. No one will ever love me."

I sigh. "Then why do you keep having sex with them?"

"*SHHH!!*" She clamps her hand over my mouth.

"Sorry," I whisper. "But . . . don't you think you should think about that?"

She looks down at her tasteless noodles. "Yeah."

Shoes click in the hallway. Ellie automatically sits up straighter.

"You girls all finished?" Ellie's mom asks, coming back into the room.

I stand up to clear my plate, but she quickly takes it from me, as if she doesn't trust me to carry it to the sink.

"Thank you," I say. But she already has her back to me as she heads to the dishwasher.

I follow Ellie to the front door.

"Are you going to be OK?" I ask. She looks so tired and sad. I know I should say something to make her feel better, but I can't think what.

She nods halfheartedly. "Thanks for being with me today," she says.

"That's what friends are for." I give her a hug and whisper in her ear. "Forget him. Forget all of them."

She nods again, but when I leave, I can almost feel her crumple behind me.

I take the long way home so I can walk by the park again. I get on my swing and pump my legs as hard as I can. It's getting dark, and the wind on my face is much colder than it was this morning. I keep pumping, going higher and higher. I whiz past the swing next to me, Ellie's swing, making it sway a little. I wish she were back here, swinging and laughing like nothing else mattered.

We used to laugh constantly. We painted each other's toenails and traded flavored lip gloss. We teased each other about who we had crushes on and practiced kissing the backs of our hands. We talked about what our first time would be like— where we'd want to do it and what our perfect men would look like. We talked about how magical it would be.

But then Ellie went and did it for real, and it seems like sex wasn't any of those things we'd imagined. I wish I could cling to what Ava says. How sex is amazing. But looking at Ellie, it's hard to believe.

To be totally honest, I've never even seen a real penis except when I was eight and my disgusting cousin, also eight, whipped his thing out and chased me around the yard. A few years ago, my mom and dad wanted to have "the talk" with me. They even had a book to show me. I was so embarrassed that I told them Ava had already filled me in on everything I needed to know. Of course, I was dying to look at that book. But with my mom and dad looking on? Uh—no.

I stop swinging and walk over to the park's poor excuse for a seesaw, the kind where you can't get hurt if your so-called friend jumps off to make you go crashing down. They've attached these springs to the bottom so the seesaw automatically balances and you can actually ride on it by yourself.

I straddle the seat and sink slowly until both feet touch the ground, then I push off. I bounce up and come back down again softly. It's dusk, and there isn't anyone else around except some old lady with two little kids. She pushes them on the merry-go-round and tells them a million times to hold on tight.

She notices me watching and gives me a questioning look, like, *What are you doing out here all by yourself?* I glance around at the empty place. The slide is becoming a shadow. Ellie's and my swings sway gently back and forth, as if two ghost friends are riding them. I get the shivers and decide I better go.

"Hey, Corinne," a quiet voice says behind me.

I nearly fall off the seesaw.

I turn and see Caleb, looking shy, his hands jammed into his jeans pockets. My stomach does a little flip-flop butterfly thing. That hasn't happened since last year's crush on Brad Stevens, who made me practically faint every time I got near him. But *Caleb?*

"You scared me," I say.

"Sorry." When our eyes meet, I swear my stomach flutters again.

"It's OK." I try not to stare at him. I tried to tell Ellie he seemed to have gotten cuter this year, but she wouldn't listen. Figures she's not attracted to the one guy who might actually treat her right. I mean, the guy's been crushing on her since we were kids. I can't imagine what it would be like to get the attention Ellie gets. Just once I'd like to get one of the flirty looks she gets every day.

Caleb studies the wood chips at his feet.

"So, uh, what are you doing here?" he asks the wood chips.

"Um . . ."

What *am* I doing here? I'm sixteen and I've been discovered by a cute guy riding on a seesaw. By myself. In the dark. On a Saturday night. There's really no good answer.

"Just thinking," I finally say. "Want to ride with me?"

"Um, sure." He walks to the other end of the seesaw and climbs on. He slowly pushes off with his feet. His curly hair looks like a fuzzy shadow in the gray light.

"I heard you were at the park earlier today. You and Ellie?"

"Yeah. Did Josh tell you?"

"Yeah."

I don't know how much he knows, but I assume Josh gives a lot more details than Ellie does, so he probably knows more than me. I push my feet against the ground lightly. It would be really great to change the subject right about now.

"So, is Ellie, you know, OK?"

I stop the seesaw with my legs, and our eyes meet. I wait, trying to figure out how to answer. But there's really nothing I can say. I kick off the ground again, and we ride up and down in silence. After a while, the little old lady says loudly enough so we hear how it's very late and they have to go home because the park isn't safe at night.

The funny thing is, with Caleb, I do feel safe. For some reason, being here in the dark with him, I don't feel scared at all.

chapter 9
Ellie

THE FIRST BOY made me feel like I was the most beautiful girl in school. He told me I was special. That he couldn't believe he was with me. When he held me, I felt like a present he didn't want to share. He said it was his first time, too. But his kisses got harder and harder. And his hands moved everywhere, too fast. A noise came out of me when he ripped his way inside me. He didn't notice. He just moaned louder.

But I wasn't moaning. I was crying. He didn't even kiss me good-bye when he was done.

I stayed after he left the room. I sat and listened to the party noises in the other part of the house we were in. To people laughing. I wiped my eyes and sat on the edge of the bed. I thought of the words he'd used earlier. How they filled me up and made me feel wanted and alive. But how, when he pushed his way inside me, he emptied me out again.

Pretty soon Corinne found me. She asked if I was all right. She wanted to know what happened. She wanted to know all the details. "Far, farther, or farthest?" she kept asking.

She giggled when I told her farthest. She jumped up and down on the bed.

"Tell me what it was like!"

But I couldn't. I wanted to be able to tell her it was the way it was supposed to be. Special. But it wasn't. And I couldn't lie. So I just shrugged and said I'd tell her later.

When I got home and changed, I saw the blood on my panties. I was afraid something was wrong with me. I called Corinne the next morning. She said that happens when you do it the first time. Her sister told her about it. Ava said that in some cultures, they check the wedding couple's sheets for blood to prove that the bride was a virgin. I couldn't stop thinking about that. About someone else seeing my blood. And knowing what I'd done.

I didn't know what to do with my bloody panties. I folded them into a tight ball and hid them way back in my under-wear drawer where I couldn't see them.

The second time, I should have known. I should have recognized the familiar lies.

You're so hot. I have to have you. C'mon . . .

And the third time.

And the fourth.

Their hands felt so good, wanting me. Needing me. Their words made me feel beautiful. Irresistible. Even powerful for that one brief moment before it was over.

But I was none of those things.

I was nothing.

Just a smell on their hands to share with their friends.

chapter 10

Caleb

"CALEB?" Corinne pushes her way toward me through the crowded hallway at school. When she catches up, she gives me a quick semi-smile.

"Hey," I say, grinning back at her.

"Hey. Thanks for hanging out with me at the park the other night."

It's just before first period, but her hair is already falling out of her hair clip. Loose curls are wispy around her face. I can't believe I never noticed how cute she is.

"No problem," I say. "Not that I was the best company."

"Well, it was nice not to be alone." She looks at her feet, then down the hall toward our homeroom.

When our eyes meet again, I take a deep breath. "Um. So. Maybe we could go again sometime."

She nods. "Yeah. Cool."

"Great!" I feel my cheeks get hot. "I mean. OK. Good."

Ugh.

I follow her to homeroom. When we get there, Corinne sits at her usual place next to Ellie, and I sit in my usual place in the back. From my seat, I watch them lean toward each other to talk. Corinne reaches over and touches Ellie's arm, as if she's trying to comfort her, but Ellie pulls away. When she turns, I see her face. She looks like she's going to cry. I don't know what they're talking about, but I think I can guess.

I don't see Josh until last period, when we have soccer. I manage to avoid him in the locker room because we're all in a hurry to get out on the floor before the coach comes in and starts yelling at us.

We get put on the same scrimmage team, but I refuse to pass to him. I don't even look at him.

After practice, I try to get out of there fast, but he comes rushing over to me.

"What was wrong with you out there? You cost us two goals!"

I turn away from him and throw my stuff together.

"Hey, what's your problem, man?"

"Nothing," I say. "Not here."

"Yeah, here. What's up with you?"

The other guys wait for a fight like vultures. Only Dave seems uncomfortable. The three of us have known each other forever, and we've never gotten in each other's faces. Never.

"I said not here." I turn away from him and grab my bag.

"Party at my house this weekend," Kyle says, walking over to Josh.

"Cool," says Dave.

"Gonna hook up with Ellie again, Josh?" Ben asks.

"Nah," Josh says quietly.

Dave looks toward me. "Cay?"

"Screw you," I say.

"What the hell? What did I say?"

I grab my stuff and push past them and head out to the parking lot. I'm halfway to my car when Josh catches up.

"Hey!"

I don't turn around.

He steps in front of me and blocks my way. "What's your problem?"

His chest is in my face.

"What happened to you?" I say.

"What do you mean?"

"You and Ellie? Come on, Josh. You're not like those ass-holes. Why do you have to talk about her like she's a piece of meat?"

"What? I don't! I just—c'mon, Cay. You know it's just bullshit. Those guys have been on my case for months."

"So you screw Ellie just so you can get those guys off your back?"

"*No*! That's not what I meant."

"What *did* you mean then?"

"I don't know! God, Cay. What do you care?"

I shake my head. "Just forget it."

"No way! You started this."

"Fine, then tell me what *really* happened with Ellie."

"You know what happened."

"Not the details. I mean, what happened between you two?"

He sighs. "Nothing. We did it. That's all."

"That's *all*?"

He looks around to make sure no one can hear. "Yeah. I mean, maybe it wasn't as great as I let on, all right? It was my first time. Why do you care so much, anyway?"

"We've known Ellie since, like, first grade, you know? The way you guys talk about her . . . it's not cool."

"I know," he says quietly. "I don't mean it. I just can't tell them what it was really like."

"Why not?"

"Because it *sucked*? I dunno. I was clueless. As soon as it was over, I took off."

"Damn, Josh. What the hell?"

"I know I'm a shit, OK? What else do you want? I screwed up."

His eyes are glassy, like he might actually cry.

"Nothing," I say. "Forget it. Just—shut up about her from now on, all right?"

"Yeah, man. OK."

"You want a ride?"

He heads to the passenger side of my car without answering and gets in.

We drive toward his house without talking. Josh turns up the stereo and pretends to be into the music, but he seems nervous to me. Like he's thinking about what happened that night. Like he can't get it out of his mind.

part two

DECEMBER

chapter 11

Ellie

I MARK ANOTHER BLACK DOT on my calendar. A speck on the white square that only I would notice. Twenty-eight days from the last day it should have come. Three months in a row. I touch the dot with my finger. It smudges on the glossy calendar paper and onto my fingertip.

Downstairs, my mother is making breakfast. The dishes clink softly. She's humming, as if everything is fine.

I start downstairs, but the smell of scrambled eggs sends me rushing to the bathroom. There isn't much to throw up. My mouth tastes sour after, and the smell makes me retch again. But there's nothing left inside me. I splash cold water on my face and bury it in a washcloth.

Corinne said she would go with me to buy a test. To be sure. But I told her I am sure. She said she'll help me find a place to go to take care of it. That we can take a bus to the city if we have to. She says her sister will help us. Ava knows what to do. And she thinks Josh will pay. But I don't want Ava to know. I don't want Josh to know. No one can know.

I brush my teeth and go back to my room. I shut the door. Shut out the smells and my mother's happy breakfast noises as she gets ready to fill us up on scrambled eggs and whole-wheat toast with jam. All our lives, she's tried to stuff us with her goodness. So why have I always felt so empty?

Way back in my underwear drawer, I reach for them. The white cotton panties I wore that first time. I carefully unfold them, like a flower opening up. But inside is the dried-up blood that proved it was my first time. It looks brownish now, and ugly. Not like a flower at all. I refold them and push them back to their hiding spot.

I don't know why I have to look. I don't know why I keep them.

"Breakfast! You'll be late if you all don't get down here now!" my mom half sings, like an orange-juice-commercial mom.

My brother's heavy footsteps thud down the carpeted stairs. My father mutters something about college behind him. His steps are quiet and careful in his dress shoes.

"Won't have anyone to cook for you next year," he jokes to my brother. He's so proud, or maybe just relieved, that Luke is applying to colleges. Luke probably rolls his eyes when my father isn't looking. He's probably stoned already. I think I smelled his sweet smoke when I woke up. The smell my parents are too naïve to know is not incense. Luke thinks it's funny, how clueless they are.

I wait in my room, afraid that if I open my door the kitchen smell will be stronger and I'll be sick again. Just hang on, I tell myself. It will be over soon. Corinne will help me.

"Ellie, you're late! Hurry up!"

I can't imagine what she'd do if she knew just how late I was. That I have shattered her good-girl dreams for me.

I'm not angry. I'm disappointed, I can hear her say if she found out. We don't get angry in this house. Especially not my mom.

And that is so much worse.

So all I can do is scream into my pillow at night so no one can hear. I pound my fists into the soft down as hard as I can.

I take one more deep breath, wipe my face again, and walk downstairs, as if nothing is wrong. Just me running late.

chapter 12

Josh

IT'S RAINING; IT'S POURING. THE OLD MAN IS SNORING.

I hear my own kid voice in my head as I listen to him out there, sleeping on the living-room couch. Again.

He says the winter depresses him. No one gets their car detailed in the winter, so he has to get by working extra hours on the regular fix-it tune-up stuff, which I know makes him feel like a loser because it's not "artistic" like the painting stuff is. And really he probably is daydreaming about getting "real" music gigs instead of playing in a men's club to a bunch of guys trying to escape from their wives or their lives or whatever.

One time, when my dad and mom were actually going out someplace together, my dad came into my room and asked me to check to see if I could smell any gas or grease on him. With the amount of Old English he'd slapped on, I don't think anyone would have known if he'd stepped in dog shit, which would have been a funny thing to say to him, if he hadn't looked so nervous.

My mom doesn't help, getting her nurse's degree and making my dad feel dumb. Not that she did it on purpose, but I think he feels like now she's better than him. Sometimes I catch him scowling at the bookshelf he made for all of her nursing books. When he finished, he was so proud of how it came out. But my mom shook it a little to test how sturdy it was. Then she said she hoped it could hold all her heavy books. I saw my dad kind of sag when she said that.

The snores stop, and he coughs a few times. The couch creaks. Then the snores start up again, quiet at first, then loud and steady. Rosie's collar jingles as she resettles on the couch next to him.

I have to get out of here.

I grab my coat and head for the door, but just as I get there, the phone rings. I grab it before my dad can wake up.

"Stud-man! We're on our way over." Dave's voice is crackly on his crappy cell phone. I swear he got it out of a cereal box.

"Your old man got any beer lying around?"

"Is the pope Catholic?"

"Be there in five."

I head back to my room and throw my coat on the bed. So much for escaping.

When Dave and Caleb get here, they don't bother to knock. As soon as I hear the front door creak open, I head out to meet them and warn them to be quiet. They creep through the living room past my dad. Dave points at my dad and pretends to guzzle a drink. He elbows Caleb and covers his mouth to keep from laughing. But Caleb looks away and pretends he doesn't notice.

I jerk my head toward the kitchen, and they follow without talking. Rosie lifts her head from the foot of the couch and sniffs the air. Her tail thumps a few times. Then she puts her head back down on my dad's feet. She never leaves his side, especially when the old man's catching z's. My dad used to joke that Rosie was more loyal to him than my mom, but he stopped saying that when it started to seem true.

In the kitchen I get us each a Bud, and we head to my room.

Dave dumps himself on my bed and of course sticks those damn shoes of his right near my pillow. I know he thinks this is funny. I swat them off and motion for him to shove over so I can sit at that end. Caleb slides the chair out from my desk and sits there like he's gonna interview us or something. We don't start talking until we've had a few chugs each.

"Something bugging you, man?" I say to Dave. "You've got about five new volcanoes going there." Whenever he's stressed out he gets these huge zits, which, being Dave, he can't help picking.

He takes another drink. "Nothing. The 'rents are fighting again as usual. I wish my mom would just kick the bastard out." He plays with the tab on the can until it falls off.

Dave's dad can be a pretty big asshole, it's true. Mike's been known to use Dave's mom as a punching bag. He's given Dave some pretty bad bruises, too.

I don't really know what to say, since basically I agree, but what can I do?

Caleb just stares out the window. He's probably thinking about his own dad. That guy's been MIA practically Caleb's whole life.

I take a long drink from my beer and try to think of a way to change the subject.

Dave shrugs and drinks, too. Then Caleb starts chugging and all three of us finish our beers. We wipe our mouths with the back of our hands at the same time.

Dave lets out a huge belch and turns to Caleb. "So, what's up with you and that bitch Corinne?" he asks.

That wasn't exactly the subject I would've picked.

Caleb looks surprised, as if we haven't noticed those two talking in the halls all the time. "We're just friends," he says, squeezing his empty can. "And she's not a bitch."

Dave nods at me. "They're hooking up."

"We are not!" Caleb says, kinda loud.

I motion for him to tone it down so he doesn't wake up the old man.

"Well, we're not," he says. "We're just friends."

"That mean you're still into Ellie?"

"*What?*" Caleb's face is bright red.

"You're into Ellie?" I ask.

"No!" Caleb glares at Dave.

Dave shrugs like he doesn't really care either way. "Too bad she never comes to parties anymore. What'd you do to her, Josh? Scare her into celibracy?"

"It's *celibacy*, you idiot. And I didn't do anything to her. Jesus."

But I still keep seeing the way she looked at me that night when I left her by herself. I stand up. "Let's get outta here."

I don't know where I want to go—just away from this place. Away from talking about all this shit.

We put the empties under my bed and walk quietly to the

kitchen for more. Then we head out, holding the cans in the pockets of our jackets.

It's freezing outside.

We climb into Dave's car and crank up the heat. We drive around, playing loud music and not talking. Just drinking and thinking. Together and alone at the same time.

chapter 13

Caleb

"WHAT SHOULD WE DO?" Corinne asks me.

I'm pacing back and forth with the phone pressed hard against my ear, wishing this was a bad joke.

"Are you sure? Did she go to a doctor? Or take a test?" My palms are sweating.

"Ellie says she just knows."

"But—how did it happen? Didn't they use anything?"

"Ellie thinks the condom slipped off or broke. She said she could feel—you know. Stuff. After. Like—"

"I get it. I get it. I don't need the details." I press my palm against my forehead and squeeze my eyes shut.

"When will she tell Josh?" I ask.

Corinne sighs. "Forget about Josh, OK? Ellie doesn't want him to know."

"But don't you think he—"

"Caleb, focus. What he doesn't know won't hurt him. Besides, we have to get Ellie to take care of it. Soon."

"Maybe if we told Josh, he could help. I mean, he could at least pay—"

"You think Josh cares?"

"He would if he knew! God, Corinne. He's not as bad as you think he is."

"Whatever. Look. If she's just going to get rid of it, why tell him? Wouldn't he be better off never knowing? Not that I care, by the way. I don't think he deserves anything, after what he did to Ellie."

I stop pacing. "What do you mean, 'what he did to her'?"

She sighs again. "Uh, he *used* her? Like all those other losers? All Ellie wanted was a boyfriend. Someone who actually cared about her. Those pricks totally took advantage of her. And Josh just left her alone outside that night. He probably didn't even notice that she never came back to the party. I'm the one who found her outside—getting sick!"

The wind rattles my window because my mom and I never got around to replacing the broken storm. But I'm not cold. I'm sweating. I place my hand on the frosty glass to stop the noise.

"Josh told me that he freaked out," I say. "He—he said he was embarrassed after. He didn't mean to leave her." But I know how lame I sound.

"Just forget it," Corinne says. "We need to focus on the current situation."

I take my hand away from the glass, leaving a clear print where I melted the frost. I curl my wet fingers into my palm and make a fist. Why did Josh have to be so *stupid*?

"I'm off to class!" my mom calls from the other side of my door. "Be back later!"

I don't bother to answer.

"Is your mom going out?" Corinne asks.

"Yeah. She's teaching an art class tonight. Why?"

"I thought I could come over." She sounds a little nervous. "To talk."

"Uh, sure." I look around at my messy room. I'm sure the rest of the house isn't in much better shape. "When?"

"How about now?"

"Um, OK."

"Great. See you soon."

I hang up after she clicks off. I should probably race downstairs to pick up the house, but instead I sit down on the edge of my bed and look out the window. It's gray outside and getting dark. We're supposed to get our first snow tonight.

I get up and go to the bookcase. I reach behind the old Narnia books and feel around until my fingers touch Ellie's old Porsche. It's dusty, and smaller than I remember. I turn it over in my hands and open the small doors, like I used to do when I was little. I remember the day Ellie gave it to me, like it was no big deal. She just smiled at me and said I could have it. I didn't even offer her anything in return. She did it just to be nice.

The wind rattles the window again. My handprint is already frosting up. I put the car back in its hiding spot and go downstairs to wait for Corinne.

chapter 14

Corinne

WHEN I DRIVE PAST ELLIE'S HOUSE on my way to Caleb's, I slow way down. This isn't right, going over to Caleb's to talk about Ellie. If I really want to help, I should take her with me. I pull over and call.

"I'm coming to get you," I say.

"Why?"

"Because. Now get ready. I'm going to be at the door in like one minute."

Ellie's mom looks surprised to see me when she opens the door.

"Corinne! We haven't seen you in ages!" She actually touches my arm. "Ellie! It's Corinne!"

Things must be really bad here if Ellie's mother is this happy to see me.

Ellie surfaces at the top of the stairs. She walks slowly. She looks pale.

Her mom looks at me expectantly, as if I'm going to make everything better. She obviously doesn't have a clue what's really bothering Ellie, though it's clear she knows *something's* wrong.

When Ellie finally makes it down the stairs, I practically put her coat on for her as we walk out the door to the car. Her mother waves at us as if we're going to the prom and I am Ellie's dream date. I force myself to smile and wave back.

Ellie rolls down the window as we pull out of the driveway. I forgot to air out my mom's car on the way over, and it smells like an ashtray. Spits of snow sprinkle the windshield and dart into Ellie's open window, but she doesn't seem to notice.

"Are you going to tell me where you're taking me?" she finally asks.

"It's a surprise."

"Why?"

"'Cause you need cheering up."

"I need more than that."

"I know."

We drive in silence, letting the heater blow hot air at our

faces, until I find Caleb's street. It's a side street, walking distance from the park, just like all of our houses. I used to say Ellie's name really loudly whenever we passed Caleb's house to embarrass her because we knew Caleb had a crush on her. We thought that was so funny back then.

Back then. It was only last summer.

Caleb's house is tall and narrow. Strings of colored lights all around the porch give it a warm glow.

When we pull into the driveway, Ellie sits forward and looks over the dash. "This is Caleb's house."

"Yup. This is your surprise."

She sits back in her seat. "I don't get it."

"I like him. I mean, not *like* him, like him. Just, you know, as friends. Since my house is lame, and we can't hang out at your house, and the park is too cold, I figured this was the next best place."

Ellie rolls her eyes. "I want to go home."

"Not a choice," I say. I get out of the car. Ellie stays put, so I go around to the other side and open her door. Now I really feel like her date.

"Come *on*," I say, and drag her out.

Caleb opens the door before we even knock. He jumps when he sees Ellie.

"Hi!" he says nervously. He looks at Ellie as if she's one of those breakable ornaments he shouldn't touch.

"Decided to bring a date," I tell him.

"Cool," Caleb says. "Hey."

Ellie gives him a bashful smile.

"Come on in."

The house smells like homemade bread. Caleb takes our coats, and we follow him into a tiny living room. There are so many paintings, you can hardly see the walls. There are canvases without frames, some just different shades of the same color, mostly blue.

Above the couch, there's a painting of a pair of hands cupped together in the shape of a heart. Coming out of them is the head of a little curly-haired cherub. I step closer to look. The cherub looks like Caleb. I bet the hands are his mom's.

In the corner is another portrait of a man. All his features are distorted, like a Picasso. He has a faraway look on his face. His mouth is closed, and in the corner there's a small hand reaching out to him, but it's like he doesn't see it. Ellie comes up behind me and looks at him, too. There's something about his eyes that makes you not want to look away.

Caleb notices us staring. "Want to sit? Something to drink?" he asks.

"Who is he?" Ellie asks quietly.

"Just some guy my mom knew," Caleb says. He fidgets nervously with the seam of his T-shirt. "Want some hot chocolate or something?"

"Do I smell bread?" I ask. Something about the painting is clearly bothering him.

Ellie starts to reach her hand toward the man's face.

"Yeah, fresh bread in the kitchen," he says.

I put my arm around Ellie and steer her away. We follow Caleb into the kitchen, which is small and crowded. There's an island in the middle with bright-colored pots hanging overhead. We sit at stools around the island while Caleb gets the bread out of a bread maker. It smells even better close up.

He's about to cut a slice when the front door opens. A tall, thin woman carrying a portfolio struggles into the hall.

"Hello?" she calls.

"In here," Caleb says. "Why are you back so early?"

"Snow," she says. "You know how my car is in this stuff. I didn't want to wait for the roads to get worse." She pulls off a long wool coat as she comes toward us and drapes it over a chair. There are specks of blue paint on her cheek and even in her spiky hair. But even though she's messy, there's a touch of elegance about her. She's wearing a black turtleneck and paint-spattered jeans.

"This is my mom, Liz," Caleb says. "You remember, Ellie, Mom. And this is Corinne."

"Lovely to meet you," she says. "Ellie, I haven't seen you in a million years! You're all grown up!"

Ellie blushes. "It's nice to see you again," she says.

"You girls have all-wheel drive? I'd hate to see you driving in this stuff."

"Oh, it's no problem," I say. "My mom's car is great in the snow."

She nods, then eyes the bread. "Here, let me fix that the right way for you. It's my specialty." She steps past us and grabs a stick of butter out of the fridge. Then she reaches for a tiny red pot from the rack above us. She melts the butter on the stove while Caleb cuts thick slices of the cinnamon raisin bread and puts them on plates for all of us. When the butter melts, Liz pours it over the bread, then sprinkles cinnamon sugar over the top. The sugar turns dark brown as it sinks into the butter.

"Dig in," she says, sliding plates at us.

The warm butter and cinnamon melt the bread in my mouth. I don't want to swallow, it tastes so good. I only once, very briefly, think about looking like a pig in front of Caleb.

Ellie keeps smiling at Caleb's mom while we eat. It's the first time I've seen her look happy in months. Her cheeks are pink, and wisps from her ponytail settle across her face in this pretty way that—I can't help it—makes me feel kind of jealous.

When we're full, we go back to the living room. Liz sits cross-legged on their deep purple couch, right under the cherub painting. She pats the space next to her, and Ellie takes it. I sit in the only other chair available, so Caleb takes the floor.

"It's so nice to have company," Liz says. "Caleb doesn't bring friends home very often."

Poor Caleb looks like he wants to hide under the coffee table.

Liz asks us about a hundred questions. We tell her how Ellie and I have been best friends since the second grade, and how we all have homeroom together. How we can't stand our history teacher because he makes us read *Time* magazine every week and gives us a quiz on it. Liz scoffs and tells us we should be reading *The Nation*. Caleb asks her not to start.

Liz feels like the aunt I always wish I had. We barely know her, but I feel like I could tell her anything. She's the kind of person who looks at you when you're talking and asks you questions as if she really cares.

By the time there's a lull in the conversation, it's time to go. Liz and Caleb are walking us to the door when Liz suddenly shrieks happily. "I almost forgot! Our first snow! And we have company. Perfect!"

She reaches for her coat and elbows Caleb to do the same. Ellie and I are already in ours.

"Not now. Please." Caleb turns red. I've never seen anyone blush as much as he does. Even his earlobes turn a deep pink.

"Oh, come on. It's tradition! We can't ignore the first snow—it's bad luck!"

"*Later,*" he whispers. But we're all standing way too close for secrets.

"Out!" she yells, herding us through the door.

Outside, there's a fresh white blanket of snow. We climb down the porch steps carefully. Liz scans the yard and points to a corner. "You there," she says to Caleb. "Ellie, you go over by the sycamore. Corinne, you go over by the rosebush."

It's a good thing she points to it, because all I can make out is this stubby-looking thing covered with snow sticking out of the ground.

She's directed us into a big triangle. She walks into the center of it, slowly sinks down onto her butt, leans back, and makes an angel, flapping her long arms and legs in the snow. Ellie and I stare in amazement while Caleb looks at us kind of apologetically.

"Down! All of you!" she orders. We obey. The snow sneaks into the neck of my jacket, but instead of being annoyed by it—which, believe me, under normal circumstances I would be—I'm thrilled. It's like an ice cube down your back on a hot day.

Then I hear laughing. Ellie is actually laughing!

I flap my arms harder, as if I'm about to take off into the night. Huge, delicate snowflakes fall onto my cheeks. I stick out my tongue and let them melt into me.

When we sit up, we're covered with white and we laugh some more.

"Happy now?" Caleb asks.

"Yes," Liz says. "Now we'll all make it through the winter."

We stand up and inspect our angels. The heads point in different directions, forming a sort of giant snowflake.

"Drive carefully, girls." Liz turns and walks back into the house.

Caleb says good night, too. He looks so cute with his hands stuffed in his pockets, his curly hair filled with snowflakes. If Ellie wasn't here, I might do something about it. I'm not sure what.

But he looks at Ellie instead of me when he says good night. Figures. They always want Ellie.

But then he walks over to me after all. My stomach flutters.

I try to look pretty while wondering what this romp in the snow has done to my frizzy hair.

"Thanks for bringing her," he says.

Oh. So much for the flutters.

"I mean, I'm glad you came." He steps a little closer. Ellie is already heading for the car. "I mean, it was nice of you to bring her, that's all. You're a good friend. To her." He steps even closer. One more step and we'll definitely be touching.

"This isn't coming out right. Sorry." His cheeks are all blushy again.

"What are you trying to say?"

Ugh. Did that sound pushy?

"Um. Come back again. And you don't have to bring Ellie."

"OK!" I say, trying not to sound too excited and most likely failing. I would like to grab him and kiss him at least on the cheek, but I haven't practiced for a while and I want any kisses I give to be just right. Especially the first one.

I smile my most practiced please-think-I'm-cute smile, pray I don't have any raisin bits between my teeth, and turn away from him, stepping in the footprints Ellie left in the snow. When I get to the car, I look back and see Caleb doing the same thing in the prints his mom left. I stick out my tongue again and let a few of these magic snowflakes land on it.

Ellie and I don't talk on the way home. I'm not sure what happened tonight, but I don't want this feeling to go away. I wonder if Ellie is having the same thought—that speaking will break this spell. We watch the snow come down on the windshield and stay in our own dreams.

Just before we get to Ellie's house, I glance over at her. She's staring out the window, one hand resting on her flat stomach.

Caleb's mom seems like a smart woman. I hope she's right. I hope we do all make it through the winter.

chapter 15

Ellie

MY MOTHER AND FATHER are downstairs watching TV. Luke is down the hall in his room, listening to the Dead with his girlfriend, Maya. I wonder if they have sex. Probably. I bet it's the good kind—the loving, gentle kind. I can tell by the way they are together. When I watch Maya, I know she's happy to be with him. When they're together, they touch without even knowing it. Like their bodies are each other's and their own at the same time. I wish I knew what that felt like.

I pull up my shirt and touch my stomach where the baby is. I push down with my finger. I don't think it can feel me, but I push again anyway.

Hello? Is anybody there?

Caleb's mom touches him all the time. So much he doesn't seem to notice. Her fingers thrum across his arm as she passes by, her hand rubs his back when she stands next to him, telling him she's there without using words. It must feel good, being touched like that. I can't remember the last time my mom or dad touched me.

Liz seems like the kind of person who listens, too. Like she wants to hear what you have to say, instead of wanting you to say only what she wants to hear. I hardly know Liz, but there was this way she looked at me that made me feel as though she could see right inside me. I wish I could call her and talk to her about everything that's happened. How the boys I was with made me feel so special at first. Like I was wanted. Me.

You're beautiful. I have to have you. You feel too good. I can't stop.

I wish I could tell her I know now how stupid I was. How I saw them all talking about me at the last party. How they tried to smell me on his hands and how I threw up behind the van, only nothing came out and it didn't get rid of that nasty feeling.

I wish I could call her and tell her how when I got home, I used a whole roll of that sticky lint-remover to get the dog hair off my clothes. How I haven't worn them since that night and won't ever again, even though they were new and it took me five stores to find them—they fit me just right and were the perfect amount of faded in all the right places and even skinny Corinne was jealous.

I wish I could tell her how every time I see any of those boys in the hall now, I have to run to the bathroom to get sick. Only until now, until I ate her wonderful bread, I hadn't eaten enough to throw up, so only slimy mucus came out and I had to spit hard to get it out of my mouth.

I wish I could tell her how I have to wait for everyone in the bathroom to leave before I can come out so no one will know it was me getting sick in there. How I just want to cry but I can't, because if I start, I know that I will never stop.

I wish I could call and tell her what's really wrong. That I need help.

But Luke knocks on my door and asks if he can have the phone. Maya's cell died, and she needs to call her friend Sky about homework. He grins at me because we both know that Sky is who they get their stash from, and soon he'll be high and everything will be better for him. He doesn't notice that I'm not smiling back. He doesn't know that inside me there's this baby and that pretty soon I'm going to get rid of it. And no one besides Corinne will ever know the baby existed. He just happily takes the phone from me.

So I can't call Liz. I can't call and tell her what's happening to me.

I can't call and ask her what I should do.

I can't.

chapter 16

Josh

"BANG ANYONE LATELY?" Kyle looks at me with a shit-eating grin. The locker room is hot and wet and smells like Dave's feet, as usual.

"What's it to you?" I say. I'm so tired of this routine.

Kyle shrugs. He's still sweating, even though he already showered. He sprays some deodorant under his arms. I step back. I don't know what brand it is, but it smells like one of those lame air fresheners my dad puts in the cars he works on to thank customers for giving him business.

"Well, if you're interested, there's a party at Ben's this weekend." He turns away from me and opens his locker. It's totally organized. His regular clothes hang perfectly from the hooks, not all bunched in a heap like mine.

"Cool," I say. But I know I won't go.

Lately it's like I'm living in some kind of dream. I'm walking down this hallway, and there are things happening behind the doors I pass. The people inside see me, but I only stop for a second to look in, then keep moving.

There's my dad, talking on the phone with Mike, having the same conversation they've had every Saturday since I can remember. Even though he's laughing, he looks sad. Like he's given up on himself.

Then there's Dave and the other guys in the locker room, pushing each other around, kidding about who they've felt up and fingered and who they still haven't but wish they could.

And Caleb, giving me that *I know the real you* look.

There's my mom in the kitchen, rushing to work every morning. She looks like she wants to say something to me, but instead she just turns away and hurries out the door.

And finally there's the room I don't look in at all. The one with Ellie in it. I rush right by that one.

"Don't forget the party," Kyle says as he slams his locker shut.

"Yeah," I say. I pick up my stuff and wonder again if I should just quit soccer to avoid all this bullshit. I could take a study hall instead. I could use it to pick up my grades, because

I am definitely getting out of this hellhole as soon as I graduate.

The instructor in my Intro to Architecture course told me I was good. Teachers never tell me that shit. So, who knows? Maybe I could actually go to college and escape.

When I get home, the house is empty. There's a message on the machine from my mom. She's working late again and says there's money on the table for takeout, only when I look, there's nothing there, which means my dad took the money to buy beer for himself and a crappy pizza from the cheap place down the street instead of something I would want, like Chinese.

Before I decide if I should wait for him to get back or just take off, the phone rings.

"Josh?"

My mom's voice sounds a little nervous. She's probably wondering if I'm mad at her for blowing us off again.

"I'm sorry I can't be home tonight, honey. Did you get the money I left?"

I don't want to be mad at her. I can't really blame her for not wanting to spend time in this cave of a house.

"Yeah," I lie. "Thanks."

"Honey, maybe we could go out for lunch on Sunday. Your dad and Mike will be watching the game together. Or . . ." Her voice trails off, but I know what she was going to say. He'd be too tired. "It could be just you and me. Wouldn't that be nice?"

Yeah. That *would* be nice. But it won't happen. Sundays are her volunteer days. Which means she'll want me to go to the soup kitchen with her first.

"You're busy Sundays, Mom. Remember?"

"Well, yes. I thought we could go to the soup kitchen together and then go out after. Just like old times."

I knew it. I knew she wouldn't give up her routine for me. She has to save everyone.

"I kind of have plans with Caleb," I lie.

"Oh. Well, just thought I'd try." She attempts to sound cheerful but doesn't pull it off. I squeeze the phone tighter.

"Sorry," I say. "Maybe we could go next week."

"Really?"

"Yeah. Why not?" But we both know not to get our hopes up.

"OK, honey. Get something good to eat tonight, all right?"

"Sure, Mom."

After we hang up, I sit at the dining-room table, looking out the window across the yard to the house on the other side of the street. There's this little old couple that lives there. Whenever they leave their house, Mr. Kestler holds his wife's elbow and leads her to the car. He opens the door for her and helps her in before hobbling over to his side and slowly backing the car out of the driveway.

I try to imagine my own parents when they're that age, my dad helping my mom into the car. But I just can't see it. I just can't see them together like that. I can't even remember the last time I saw them touch each other. It's hard to believe they ever did.

chapter 17

Corinne

THE LIGHT AT ELLIE'S FRONT DOOR has a motion sensor, so it doesn't turn on until you get a few yards away. It always freaks me out. Like I'm suddenly onstage for the whole neighborhood to see, when a second before I felt like a prowler going up to their dark house.

The door opens before I knock, and there's Ellie's mom ready to welcome her daughter's savior.

"Corinne!" she says. "Ellie's on her way down. It's so good to see you." But I swear what she really means is, *Oh, thank God you're here. Quick, take my troubled daughter and make her better. I know in normal circumstances I would hope for a more appropriate friend for her, but as things are a bit desperate, I'll take you.*

Ellie's family is so messed up. It's like they don't even know how to talk to each other except to say robot family phrases. *How was your day? How was work? Pass the peas. Dinner was delicious.* I don't know how Ellie can stand it. My parents are the total opposite, which can be kind of a pain, but at least it shows they care.

"Hi," Ellie calls from the top of the stairs. She's always coming from her bedroom. I wonder if she ever goes in any other rooms in the house. Once, when we were little, I convinced her to play in the living room while her mom was busy outside, and Ellie went nuts when she saw we'd left footprints in the carpet. She actually made me help her wipe them out with our hands as we crawled backward out of the room. The carpet in my house is so old and worn that until that day, I didn't even know you *could* leave footprints on a rug.

Ellie puts on her coat and says good-bye to her mother, who tells me to drive carefully. Guess I'm Miss Ellie's date again.

"Think we'll get fresh bread tonight?" I ask as we pull out of the driveway.

"Hope so."

I nod. This would be a good time to bring up Ellie's problem. But I don't know where to start. I looked some stuff up on the Web and found out that she needs to do something soon. Really soon.

"So," I say. "We need to talk about stuff."

She peeks through the crack in the open window and lets the cold air blow on her face.

"Ellie? I know it's hard. But you need to talk about what you're going to do."

She closes her eyes against the breeze.

"I'll go with you and everything. I'll find out how to get there. Just say the word."

She leans back into the seat and sighs.

"C'mon, Ellie. We've got to—"

"Not yet."

"El, I really don't think—"

"I said not yet." She leans forward and puts her face to the window again.

"OK," I say quietly. "Not yet."

When we pull into Caleb's driveway, Ellie doesn't get out of the car. "I'm scared," she says to the windshield. The colored lights from the porch cast a rainbowish glow on her face.

"Me, too," I say.

"I don't know what to do."

"We'll get through this. I'll help you."

She nods, turning her face toward the lights and the warm, glowing house.

"Come on," I say. "Let's go in."

We make our way to the front porch and ring the doorbell. Liz opens the door, and a waft of warm, cinnamon-smelling air wraps around us and pulls us inside like an invisible blanket, protecting us from the truth for one more day.

chapter 18

Caleb

CORINNE, ELLIE, AND I SIT on the floor in the living room around the coffee table and do our homework while my mom reads.

"This is absolute crap!" she huffs from behind her paper. "Goddamn conservative."

I hate it when she does her "I'm such a hip liberal" act. Ever since Ellie and Corinne started coming over, she seems to be trying way too hard to show them what a cool mom she is.

Ellie totally eats it up. She seems to get some sort of vitamin supply just from looking at my mom. And Corinne, who never seemed to care about anything but *People* and *Entertainment Weekly*, is suddenly snatching up my mom's discarded *Nation* and *Mother Jones* magazines like they're gold. I swear she has a spell over them. Since that night two weeks ago when they first came here, they've been over practically every other night. I'm not complaining about *that*. But I get the feeling that they're here more for my mom than for me.

When the phone rings, my mom peers over her paper to let me know I should answer.

"Hello?"

"Dave and I are coming to get you, Bud," Josh says. "Dave scored a bottle of vodka from his old man, and we're going to the park."

Ellie, Corinne, and my mom watch me with that *Who is it?* look.

I stand up and turn my back to them. "Um, this isn't a good time."

"What the hell? We're, like, two streets away. Don't be a wuss."

"I don't think so." I take a few steps away from the three pairs of ears I know are listening.

"You don't *think* so? Since when did you turn down a chance to get hammered?"

Their eyes burn into my back. I take the phone into the kitchen.

"My mom's been on my case about going out on school nights," I say quietly.

"Tell her you're coming over to study."

"Like she'd believe that one." But it's tempting. At least I know it's me they want to hang out with.

"OK, well, your loss," he says.

"Save some for me and we'll go out Friday."

"Yeah, right." He hangs up.

I stay in the kitchen to escape the eyes. I open the fridge and try to find something to drink besides soy milk and ginger iced tea.

"Don't fall in," Corinne whispers behind me.

I jump and hit my head.

"Sorry. Didn't mean to scare you."

I touch my head with my hand. "S'OK."

"So, who was that on the phone?"

I shrug.

"Does that mean you don't know? 'Cause I'm pretty sure you seemed to know who you were talking to."

"Can we talk about this later?" I whisper, nudging my head toward the living room.

"I can't believe you. How can you still be friends with him?" She says it loudly, like she wants Ellie to hear.

"*Will you be quiet?*" I whisper.

She glares at me and pulls her hair behind her ears.

"You don't understand. You don't know him."

She squeezes her lips together and shakes her head. "Maybe I don't know *you*." She turns and walks back into the other room.

I stay there, wondering how that just happened.

"Caleb, would you mind putting the kettle back on?" my mom calls from the other room. "We need another round."

Leave it to my mom to know I need some time to myself. She may be obnoxious sometimes, but she always seems to have my back.

I switch on the burner and watch it turn red.

There are footsteps behind me, and a clinking noise. I turn, expecting to see Corinne again. But it's Ellie, trying to balance three teacups on their saucers.

"Uh, let me help you," I say. I reach for the cups, and our fingers touch as I help her guide them to the counter. A few months ago, the thought of Ellie in the kitchen—with me—would have been a fantasy. But now it just makes me feel sad.

"Thanks," she says. "Water almost ready?"

"Yeah, I think so."

We watch the teapot as if it's going to do something interesting. It has a little bird on the spout that whistles when the water boils. I always let the whistle go for a few seconds before I take the kettle off. But right when it really starts to sing, Ellie grabs a potholder and moves the kettle like she's putting the bird out of its misery.

"Sorry," she says. "I can't stand when it screams."

"I never thought of it like that."

She shrugs.

Together, we make the new cups of tea and carry them to the living room. Corinne raises her eyebrows at me. I flash her a grin to see if she's really mad. She smiles back, just a little.

After they leave, I take the cups back to the kitchen and see the bird on its side, staring blankly from the kitchen counter. I pick it up and put it back in the spout. It's still warm and feels almost alive.

"Thanks for helping pick up," my mom says from behind me. "They're such nice girls, aren't they?"

"Yeah," I say. But when I turn around, she has a worried look on her face. She opens her mouth to say something, but stops.

"What?" I ask.

"Nothing. See you in the morning," she says. She ruffles my hair like she did when I was little, then heads off to bed.

chapter 19

Ellie

I'm AT MY LOCKER when I open my backpack and see it there, on top of my books. A small envelope with my name written in blue capital letters. I turn it over in my hands and quickly look around before tucking it between two books and rushing to homeroom.

At my desk, I gently tear open the envelope. Slowly, carefully, I pull out the folded white paper inside. I check to see if anyone's watching. They are all too busy doing their morning things. Studying last-minute and copying each other's homework. Mr. Howard hides behind his newspaper instead of taking attendance.

I unfold the paper, excited and almost afraid. I hold it tight in both hands so it won't shake. I don't recognize the neat handwriting.

> *Dearest Ellie,*
>
> *I think it's time to talk about your situation. Come over tonight for some cinnamon bread and tea. Everything will be all right. You are a special girl.*
>
> *Love,*
>
> *Liz*

The blue letters slant neatly to the right, as if they are trying to lean off the page.

I forget to cover the paper the way I had planned. I don't move at all. I just stare at the leaning words.

Liz knows my secret. She knows about my *situation*.

I feel people near me. Watching me. Watching my hands hold this note. Trying to read it over my shoulder. Watching my tears mark wobbly lines down my cheeks, like tiny brooks that drip off my jaw and onto the paper, turning the blue words into water.

Check it out.

Is she OK?

Can you see what it says?

What's wrong with her?

They lean into me to see the blurry words, as if I'm not sitting here. Maybe I'm not. Maybe this isn't happening. Maybe I'm asleep, and I'm going to wake up any minute. And my mother is going to have breakfast waiting. And we'll eat whole-wheat pancakes with Vermont maple syrup. And Luke won't be stoned. And we'll all just sit and talk about how good those pancakes are. About which schools Luke will get into and which ones I'll apply to next year. About how bright our futures are.

Someone leans closer. Chocolate doughnut breath in my face. I should hide the note. But I don't move. I don't move. I don't.

I just stare at the wet blue words running off the paper.

chapter 20

Corinne

"I THINK JOSH LIKES YOU. I saw him checking you out when you walked by him at lunch," Kayla says to Jessie.

"Oh, my God, really? Josh is so hot."

I can't stand having my locker next to the two of them. They're obsessed with who's into them. They're always at the same parties Ellie and I go to—I mean, *used* to go to—whispering behind their hands every time someone walks by them. As far as I can tell, *no one* is into them. Without thinking, I make a *hmph* noise to indicate Josh is so totally *not* hot.

"What's *your* problem?" Jessie asks.

Josh is a loser?

"Nothing," I say, slamming my locker.

"Jealous," Kayla says.

Yeah. That's it.

They laugh and turn away from me. I spot Caleb heading down the hall, so I rush to catch up.

"Can we come over tonight?" I ask.

"Sure." He smiles. I wonder if it's at the thought of me coming over or Ellie.

"She seems better, don't you think?" he asks before we get to homeroom. Guess that answers my question.

"Yeah, definitely. But"—we stop outside the door—"something has to happen soon. I'm afraid it'll be too late if she waits much longer."

"When does she have to—you know, do it by?"

"I'm not sure. Within three months or something like that?"

He frowns and peeks through the window in the door. He's looking for her. I wish I didn't feel jealous. She's my best friend, and she's a mess. The last thing I should care about is whether Caleb still has a thing for her.

What I *should* be doing is pushing her to take care of things. *Soon.*

Caleb opens the door, and we walk in. Ellie is already in her seat, reading something. She's hunched over. Her hair hangs down in front of her face.

"Hey, El, whatcha got?" I ask, trying to be friendly.

She doesn't look up.

"What is it, a death threat?" I joke.

I lean down so I can see her face. It's blotchy and wet. I peek at the letter. The words are all smudged and blurry from her tears. I gently pull the paper out of her hands and read it.

"What's going on?" Caleb asks innocently. I look into that cherub face and want to slap him. I shove the letter at him instead.

His mouth drops open as he reads. "But I didn't—" he starts.

My glare cuts him off.

Ellie looks up at me. Her eyes are glassy, questioning.

"Ellie—" I start. But I don't know what to say.

More people come into the room. I reach into my purse and luckily find some tissues. I hand one to Ellie, but she doesn't move. I try to wipe her face off, but it doesn't help because tears are still seeping out the corners of her eyes.

"She must have put it in my backpack last night," Ellie says quietly, looking down at her hands. "But . . . how does she know?"

"Come on," I say. I shake my head at Caleb.

"Corinne, I didn't—" he starts again.

I take Ellie's hand, and we leave him standing there holding the letter. Mr. Howard doesn't try to stop us.

I lead Ellie to the bathroom so I can help her wash her face. The room's empty because the homeroom bell already rang. I look for feet in the stalls just in case. When I'm sure we're alone, I lead Ellie over to the sinks.

"Are you OK?" I ask, even though I know the answer.

She nods and dabs the now-soggy tissue at her eyes.

"Ellie, I think you should go to the nurse and get her to send you home."

She sniffs and shakes her head. "What would I tell her?"

"You could tell her the truth, El. I'll go with you. We can talk to her together."

She leans against the brick wall next to the sinks and lets her head thud back on it. Her eyes are red and puffy. She closes them, but tears still sneak out.

I stand next to her so our arms are touching. I reach with my hand until I feel hers and squeeze.

"Ellie, you've got to talk to someone. There must be somebody we can go to. Maybe the school counselor."

I squeeze her hand again, looking for even a little sign that there's some life left. But she doesn't squeeze back.

I let go and feel her slip away.

"Please talk to me, El. We've got to do something about this soon. Before it's too late."

She moves forward a little so I can't see her face.

"Liz," she says quietly.

"Liz. Yeah! Of course! We'll go to her tonight. OK?"

Ellie touches her stomach. "How did she know? How could she?" She looks down at her stomach.

"No, Ellie, you can't tell." I take a deep breath. "It's my fault."

She looks at me, confused.

"I—I told Caleb. I'm *really* sorry, El. But I've been so worried about you, and I didn't know what else to do. I thought he could help. That he would want to help. I swear, Ellie. I only told him because—well, you know, El—the guy's been in love with you forever. And I don't mean the *gaga* love but the caring kind. He's worried about you, just like I am. And he *does* want to help, El. I never thought he'd tell Liz. I swear I wouldn't have told him if I thought he wouldn't keep it a secret. I guess he told her because he cares so much about you."

I didn't expect it to hurt so much to tell her that, but it does. My chest gets heavy, and my throat tightens the way it does when I try not to cry.

I step closer to her. At first I think she's going to turn and run, but she doesn't move.

"That explains a lot," she says. She doesn't seem angry. She doesn't seem anything.

"So, you're not mad?"

"No."

"And we'll go to Liz? Tonight?"

She nods.

Thank God. I give her a little hug. She doesn't hug back, but she doesn't pull away, either.

"Here, let's fix you." I empty my makeup onto the counter and tell her to face me. Then I open up my concealer and dot her face, then rub it in the way my sister taught me to. Gently, slowly. She closes her eyes and lets me do my work.

When I rub some blush on her cheeks, she opens her eyes, but she doesn't look at herself in the mirror.

"You look fabulous," I say. I reach for her hand again. It's cold in mine, but this time she squeezes back.

"It's gonna be all right," I tell her. I let go of her hand and put both of mine on her shoulders. I shake her a little, just gently.

"I promise," I say. "Remember the angels?"

"Yeah," she says.

We start to walk out, but as we pass one of the stalls, we

hear a giggle and freeze. Someone is in there. I look through the crack in the door and see them. Kayla and Jessie. They're perched on either side of the toilet seat and leaning on the stall walls. Kayla has a sports bottle in her hand and she's sucking it fast.

"Can we help you?" Jessie asks in her annoying, throaty voice that sounds like she's been smoking since she was two.

I jump back. Ellie's frozen against the wall.

Kayla laughs.

Without thinking, I kick the stall door. It swings open and bumps into one of them.

"Shit! You bitch, you made me spill!" Kayla yells. There's some red liquid on her white shirt. I'm sure it's Kool-Aid and vodka.

"I wish I'd made you fall in!" I say back, though not having the closed door between us is making me a lot less brave than I sound.

Jessie jumps down from the toilet as if she's about to pounce on us. I grab Ellie by the hand and pull her out of the room fast. We rush down the empty hall back to homeroom. Their footsteps thud behind us. Luckily they're going to have to ditch their drinks before a teacher sees them, so we're safe for now.

"Don't worry about them," I say before we go back in.

As I start to open the door, Ellie puts her hand on my arm.

"Thanks," she whispers.

We look at each other for just a second, but it's long enough for me to see that her eyes really are different. I didn't notice when I was putting on her makeup, but I see now. Or maybe it's what I don't see. Something that used to be there is gone.

Ellie follows me inside. Everyone watches us suspiciously as we walk to our seats. Even Mr. Howard glances up from his newspaper and clears his throat. I'm sure they're all dying to know what's going on. And of course it's only a matter of time before Kayla and Jessie tell them.

chapter 21

Josh

I PEEL OFF MY SWEATY T-SHIRT and throw it into my gym bag. The sooner I can get out of here the better. I'm about to take off when Kyle comes up behind us and shoves Caleb's shoulder.

"Hey, Special Cay, you stud."

It's nice to hear him giving someone else crap for a change. But Caleb? A stud?

Dave walks out of the shower naked, wiping his poor, zit-covered face with his towel. "What's he talking about?"

Caleb looks as confused as I do. "Wish I knew. Sounds good," he says.

"Kayla and Jessie overheard some interesting news in the girls' bathroom today," Kyle says. He makes this sly face, like he's got some huge secret. Jesus, he's such a dick. Sometimes I don't know what I want to do more: laugh at him or kick his ass.

"They were talking about *me*?" Caleb asks.

"About you and someone else," Kyle says.

"Damn, Cay, you keeping something from us?" I ask.

"Not that I know of, but I'm dying to hear what I did." He sounds nervous.

Dave, the sex-crazed lunatic, runs over to Caleb. Even though he's still naked, he starts giving Caleb this noogie like he's gonna rub the guy's hair right off and make a premature bald spot.

"Cut the shit!" Caleb yells.

"Whoa!" Dave backs off and puts a towel around himself.

Kyle laughs. "Touchy much?"

"Just tell me what you're talking about," Caleb says. He looks like he's about to beat the crap out of Kyle.

"OK, OK. God. I heard about you and Ellie, all right? I didn't know you were so sensitive, dude. But damn, you should've asked us for some advice on keeping your soldiers behind enemy lines before you went all the way."

Caleb is totally pale.

"Wait," I say, starting to register what Kyle just said. "You were with *Ellie*?"

Kyle nods. "All the way, man." He turns to Caleb. "I mean, *Daddy*."

"Whoa!" Dave steps back like Caleb has some contagious disease.

"Shut up, Kyle. I mean it." Caleb steps closer to him, as if he's about to pummel Kyle even though Kyle could flatten him in two seconds. I should step in, but I don't move. I'm hot all over. My whole body is sweating. *Daddy?* Ellie's pregnant?

"Aw, I think he's in love." Kyle laughs in Caleb's face.

"I said, shut up." Caleb curls his hands into fists.

Kyle laughs, like he knows Caleb would never try it. But as Kyle turns to say something to me, a flash of fist connects with his jaw and his head spins the other way.

"Shit!" he screams.

Caleb stands there. Frozen.

Kyle looks at him for a half second before he throws one back at him. Caleb doesn't even have time to duck. Kyle's fist connects to his mouth and knocks Caleb back so he crashes into Dave. He looks like one of those blow-up clowns you punch and make fall over, only they bounce up again for more, which is exactly what happens, and this time Kyle gets him in the gut.

"What the —?" Dave tries to get between Caleb and Kyle. It all happens in, like, three seconds and I don't even think. I shove myself in front of Kyle so Dave can drag Caleb out of range.

"You little fucker! You really are stupid," Kyle hisses at him. He spits a mouthful of blood on the floor.

Caleb looks at all of us, bright red blood already oozing out of the side of his mouth, then he grabs his bag and leaves.

"What the hell's going on?" I run out into the cold after him. "Cay! Wait up!"

"Not here," Caleb yells into the air without turning around.

"Hey!" I catch up with him and grab his shoulder, flinging him around to face me. He gives me this look. Not the crazed, mad look he gave Kyle and that I expected, but a look of pity. Like I am the most pitiful bastard in the world.

"What's going on?" I yell. But I think I know. I think I knew as soon as Kyle started talking, but I just didn't want to believe it.

He shakes his head.

"Say it."

He waits, like they are the hardest words to say and he has to use all his strength to get them out.

"It's you."

My stomach tightens. I have to swallow hard to keep from puking.

The wind whips at our faces as we stare at each other. His mouth is already swelling up. It must hurt like hell, but he doesn't seem to notice. He turns away from me and starts walking.

When we get to his beat-up Corolla, we both climb in and head for his house. We don't crank the heat or turn on the radio. We don't say a word. I look out the passenger window and watch the outskirts of our pathetic town pass by me. My dad's stupid body shop, the diner, the run-down gas station, some abandoned buildings. It's all so ugly. Even covered with snow, it's ugly.

I think I'm gonna be sick.

I bend forward and put my face in my hands, pushing my forehead against the dashboard.

This isn't happening. This isn't happening.

I keep saying it to myself until the words run together and don't make any sense. It makes me dizzy, and I lift my head and watch the still-ugly town go by.

"Shit!" I yell, breaking up the cold quiet of the car.

Caleb doesn't flinch.

"Fuck!" I smash my fist down on the armrest. The thing jiggles like it's about to break. I pound it again, and one side slides down.

Caleb turns the car onto the road that leads to our

neighborhood—past the park and to his house. When he pulls into the driveway, he cuts the motor and leans back into his seat.

"What do you know?" I ask. My breath floats out in front of me and fogs up the window.

"Not much. Corinne told me."

"How does she know it's mine?"

"Don't."

"What?"

"Don't be an asshole now, Josh. Not on top of everything else."

"What the hell? It's not like I'm the only one she did it with."

"Yeah well, you're the only one who couldn't keep your condom on, OK? You're the last guy she was with."

He looks out his window, turning his face from me. Like I'm so disgusting he can't even look at me. There's blood down the front of his T-shirt, and he's shivering without his coat.

"OK," I say. "Sorry. But in case you didn't notice, this is serious shit. I just want to be sure this is really my problem."

"It is," he says quietly. Like he doesn't want it to be true, either.

"What's she gonna do?" I ask.

"Get rid of it. What else?"

His words hang there, fogging up his side of the car.

Get rid of it.

I close my eyes and try to breathe. I rock back and forth, like my body's nodding, *Yes, it's true.* But I'm shaking my head at the same time. I feel her soft, warm body under mine, her quiet breath in my ear as I pushed inside her. She made a noise, and I hoped it meant she wanted me to be doing what I was doing, but, oh God, I didn't care—she felt so good, and then I was moving so fast and then it was over in two seconds and I know the condom fell off but I thought it happened when I was pulling out, so it was OK. But oh, God. Oh, God. I was so stupid! She didn't say anything about it. She just looked at me. And I . . . I looked away. I just left her there.

You're the last guy she was with.

"Shit!" I slam my fist on the armrest again, but it's already broken, and a screw hanging out of the door slices the side of my hand. I stare at it, waiting for the sting and the blood to surface.

Caleb groans, when it should be me.

I pull my sleeve down over my hand and hold it in a fist.

"Is she OK?" I finally ask.

Caleb doesn't answer. He doesn't have to.

"Never mind," I say. "Just tell me what I should do. How much will it cost?"

"I don't know."

He moves a little and glances over at me. The blood around his mouth has gelled up. It looks like that face paint stuff we used to wear at Halloween when we were kids. I can feel my own blood soaking my shirt.

"The thing is, she doesn't know you know. And according to Corinne, I don't think she wants you to."

"Oh."

I know this is the part when I should start feeling relieved. She doesn't want to involve me. It's not my problem. So why does my chest feel like someone just punched me with an iron fist?

"What else do you know?" I ask. "When is she going to — I mean —" I don't know why I can't say the words.

"I'm not sure. Corinne doesn't tell me that much."

"Wait a minute. How long have you known about this?"

"Relax. Not that long. Corinne told me and swore me to secrecy."

But he's still looking out that damn window and fidgeting with his key chain. He's not telling me everything.

"What the hell, Cay? *Corinne?* Why would you agree to anything that bitch says? I can't believe you're into her. You kept this from me for *her?*"

"She's not a bitch! What is it with you and Dave? You don't even know her! God, Josh. I didn't have to tell you all this, ya know."

Some fresh blood oozes out from under the stuff that's drying.

God, I'm an asshole. Everything's my fault. Everything.

"Sorry," I say. I reach in the backseat for his jacket and hand it to him. "I'm a fuckup."

"Forget it."

"How's your face?"

He touches his lip and flinches. But he smiles real fast and says, "It was worth it—that bastard."

"Thanks, man."

"I didn't do it for you."

"Right." I should have known that. "How'd that prick find out, anyway?"

He groans, then reaches into his pocket and pulls out what looks like a letter.

"Ellie had it at school. She was really upset, so Corinne took her to the girls' room to talk. I guess Kayla and Jessie overheard and blabbed to Kyle."

"What is it?"

"Read it," Caleb says, handing the paper to me.

Oh, shit. What now?

I open the folds slowly, trying not to get any blood on it. My hands are shaking so hard, I have to press the paper against my thighs to read the blurry note.

"Your *mom* knows?"

Caleb nods and looks up at the house as if she's watching us from inside. "She knows about Ellie. I don't know if she knows you're the . . . you know."

He doesn't say the word, but it's there between us anyway.

Father.

You're the father.

I lean back into the seat and try to breathe. Oh, God, please just let this be some stupid nightmare. Please let me wake up now. But I have this very real note in my hand, and when I look down again at those blurry words, I know they're probably like that because of Ellie's tears.

I crush the paper into a ball with my good hand and hold it in my fist.

"I'm outta here."

Caleb sits up a little. "Want a ride?"

"No, thanks. Sorry about the armrest. I'll take care of it."

I shut the door and leave Caleb sitting in the car. It was cold in the car, but it's twice as cold outside. I put on my jacket and throw my backpack over my shoulder. The wind rips at my face and into my ears as I walk slowly down the driveway and toward home. When I turn the corner near the park, I look out over the playground where Caleb and Dave and I first met. Where I first saw Ellie that day after it happened.

The swings and slide and other playground stuff are covered with snow. I stand there like an idiot, wondering how this all happened. Cars go by me, splashing slush at the backs of my legs. My right hand is throbbing inside my pocket. I pull my other hand out and open my fist. The note is squeezed into a tiny ball now. I hurl it over the playground fence. It lands in the snow near the merry-go-round and disappears. I'm numb but stinging all over at the same time, and all I hear is my own voice in my head. *What have I done? What have I done?*

chapter 22
Caleb

"WHY DID YOU DO IT?"

My mom's in her studio with her back to me, dabbing her brush to make leaves on a fallen tree, only the color is red instead of green.

She stops dabbing but doesn't turn around.

"What did I do?" she asks calmly.

I force myself not to grab her brush and throw it across the room. "The *note*? To *Ellie*?" My lip and jaw throb when I talk.

She sets her brush down and turns toward me on her swivel stool. She jumps when she sees me.

"What *happened*?" She starts toward me.

"Nothing. Don't get up. We have to talk."

"You're bleeding!" she says, reaching for my face.

I lean back. "I'm fine! Forget it! Just tell me about the note!"

"What note?"

"The one you gave to Ellie? The one you *shouldn't* have given to her? God, Mom. Do you have to interfere with *everything*? You act like Ellie and Corinne are your kids. They're not! They're *my* friends!"

The concern for me drains from her face. "If they're your friends, you should be trying to help them! Ellie obviously needs to talk to someone—"

"How did you know?"

"I can put two and two together. And I overheard her say something to Corinne that gave me a pretty big clue. I'm sorry. I should have talked to you first."

I sink into the chair she uses for models in the once in a hundred years she uses one. When I was little, I used to curl up in this chair and fall asleep to the rhythmic sound of her brushstrokes.

She rolls toward me on her stool. When she sees my face up close, she flinches.

"You need to get some ice on that. Who did it?"

"It doesn't matter. Stop changing the subject. You should have seen her, Mom. She looked . . . devastated. Holding that letter in her hand and crying? With everyone staring at her and thinking she was nuts?"

"I don't understand. Why did she have the note at school? I thought she'd read it at home."

"Well, you thought wrong. She read it in homeroom this morning. Corinne thinks *I* told you. She won't even talk to me."

"Oh."

"Yeah. Thanks."

"I'm sorry, honey. I was only trying to help."

"Well, you didn't."

She sags in her own stool.

"Is Josh the father?"

I look into her watery green eyes and nod.

"Everything's so messed up now," I say. "But maybe it's what Ellie needed. Maybe now she'll do something."

"Like what?"

"Get an abortion?"

She bites her bottom lip and nods. "Has she told her parents?"

"I don't know."

"What about Josh?"

"He just found out."

"How'd he take it?"

I look out the tiny window in the studio, wondering how long it took him to walk home. "He's pretty messed up."

"Poor kids," she says. She leans closer to me again. "Speaking of messed up, let's take care of your face."

But when we get up, we hear a car outside.

"It's them," I say quietly. "What should we do?"

"Let them in?"

I follow her through the door that leads back to the house and into the front hall. My mom opens the door before Ellie and Corinne reach the steps. The wind brushes their hair across their faces as they squint up toward the porch light. My mom steps back to let them in.

Ellie and Corinne glance at my face, but they don't talk to me. I take their coats and scarves. They follow my mom into the living room while I hang up their stuff. When I join them, they're sitting at their usual places: Ellie and my mom on the couch, Corinne in the chair nearby. I take my spot on the floor. When I bend down, my face throbs.

"Who wants to go first?" my mom asks quietly.

Corinne and Ellie look at their hands, the paintings, the coffee table. Pretty much everywhere but at me, my mom, or each other. I feel like I should leave, but I don't know how.

"I know this is hard," my mom finally says. "But I think we should get things out in the open so I can help you." She turns to Ellie. "I'm sorry about my note. I meant for you to read it at home. I should have written that on the envelope."

Ellie nods but stays quiet.

"And Caleb didn't tell me," my mom adds. "I just had a feeling."

Corinne looks at me guiltily.

"How far along are you?" my mom asks Ellie.

Ellie grips the edge of the couch. My mom reaches over and lays her hand over Ellie's. "You can say it out loud. Maybe that's what you need to do."

I wish I could sneak out of the room, but I'm trapped.

Ellie stares at my mom's hand on hers like it's a foreign object.

"I'm sorry, hon. You don't have to say anything if you don't want to."

Ellie pulls her hand away. She crosses her arms at her chest and shakes her head. "I don't want to talk about it. I just want it to be over. I—I want you to take me. Will you take me?"

Her mouth starts moving around in that frowny way little kids' do when they're trying not to cry.

My mom touches Ellie's shoulder. "Of course. Of course I will. But, honey. You have to tell your parents first."

Ellie nods, then hides her face in her hands. Her shoulders start to shake. A small sound comes out from behind her hands, all muffled and hidden.

My mom leans into Ellie in slow motion. She wraps her arms around her and rocks her, slowly, like she's done to me a hundred times. "It's OK. You let it out. It's OK," she says into Ellie's ear.

Corinne's crying now, too. The quiet kind of crying, when tears drip down your cheeks without anyone noticing, like my mom does when she watches sad movies.

My mom holds Ellie as if she's her own daughter. Then Corinne gets up and sits on the other side of Ellie. The three of them huddle on the couch in one big hug. I sink lower on the floor, as if I shouldn't even be witnessing this.

At this moment, I would give anything to disappear.

chapter 23

Ellie

"IT'S NOT TRUE," my mother says. She's holding a dish towel in her hands. Her knuckles are white, she's clutching it so tightly.

I'm sitting at the kitchen table. The tabletop smells like Murphy Oil Soap.

"It is," I say.

"Shut up!"

She's never said that to me before. I don't think she meant to say the words out loud. She covers her mouth with her hand as if she just said the *F* word.

I look down at the grain in the wood. I clasp and unclasp my hands in my lap.

"I'll get an abortion," I say. The word and its meaning echo in my brain. *Abortion. Abort. Terminate. End.*

My mother turns away from me and looks out the window above the sink at our snowy backyard. Our playhouse is out there. The one she and my dad gave to Luke and me for Christmas when I was in first grade and Luke was in second. Luke wanted my dad to help him build a tree house in the big oak tree at the back of the yard, but my mother said it would be unsightly. Instead she made my father order a kit from Little Victorians. My father and Luke spent a weekend assembling it. They spread all the different-size boards out on the lawn, and I helped make piles of the various screws and bolts and things they needed. As soon as the house was put together, my mom painted it the same colors as our house. Beige with white trim.

Luke said it looked like a dollhouse and refused to play in it, even though he'd spent all that time with my dad building the thing. But I spent hours alone in that house. Only in my mind I wasn't alone because I had an imaginary dog and cat, Ginger and Cocoa, to keep me company. I had tea parties with them and told them all my secret worries and dreams.

Luke and I always wanted real pets. Something warm that you could cuddle or hold on your lap. But pets are too messy. They shed. They smell. One Christmas my mother actually got us each a goldfish as a compromise. Luke and I put them in the same bowl so they wouldn't be lonely, and we took turns having them in our rooms. They swam in circles in the water, looking at me with big, pleading eyes. Bored eyes. All I could do was touch the cold glass with my finger and wait for my orange fish to swim past, brushing the side of the clear cage with its tail.

My mother sniffs. She puts her hands on the edge of the counter in front of the sink. I think she's holding herself up.

I breathe in the clean smells slowly, filling my lungs with pine scent. People always say to take a deep breath before you do something brave. It's supposed to calm your heart. But mine is beating so fast it hurts.

"Mom," I say, "I'm going to take care of this. No one has to know."

Her shoulders are shaking.

"How could this happen, Ellie?" she asks without turning around.

I don't know how to answer.

I breathe again. "You don't have to take me to the clinic. Just give me permission. Corinne will take me."

She reaches her hand to her face. I'm sure she's wiping away tears.

"How?" she says again, almost in a whisper. "You've always been a good girl."

I hear their words in my head: *You're so beautiful.*

She tips her head downward toward the sink. I bet she wishes there were some dishes to do, but she always cleans the dishes as soon as she clears the table.

"Mom?" But she still won't turn around. "I'm sorry."

I wait for her to come to me and hold me and tell me I will be OK. That *she's* sorry she didn't give me the girl talk she should have. That she's sorry she never warned me to be careful. To understand the difference between words and love. To know when to stop. To say no.

I wait for her to scream at me. To shake me and tell me what a fool I am. I wait for her to do something. Anything. *Please.*

But she stays at the sink. She doesn't look at me. She doesn't touch me.

Not even my mother can love me.

chapter 24

Corinne

IT'S BUSY WHEN WE GO BACK TO THE CLINIC for the final visit. The first time, I waited for almost two hours while Ellie got poked and prodded and tested and educated about her choices. Liz went to the exam room with her, so I had to sit by myself, watching people come in and out for reasons I could almost guess by the looks on their faces.

Today, Ellie sits between Liz and me. We wait quietly, seemingly fascinated by the purses we hold in our laps. When a nurse comes for Ellie, I stand up and give her a hug. I barely feel her hands touch my back. I want to tell her that a few months from now, this whole thing will be just a bad memory. I want to tell her she's doing the right thing. But I know she won't forget. And she wouldn't believe me. So I don't say anything at all.

I try not to look at the other women and girls waiting their turns. They know I'm here as a friend. The lucky one. Only one of the girls is here with a boyfriend. They sit across from me, holding hands. The boyfriend rubs his thumb back and forth across the top of the girl's hand in a calm rhythm. She rests her head on his shoulder. He stares straight ahead.

I have to get out of here.

It's cold outside but sunny. I lean against the brick building and close my eyes, letting the sun warm my face. On any other day, this would feel good. But today, all I can think about is Ellie. Ellie on some exam table with a hot light shining between her legs. I bet she won't say anything, even if it hurts. She'll just bite her lip and let them do whatever it is they do. My sister never told me what it was like. I wanted to ask, but then I heard her and her boyfriend crying together in her room when she came home afterward and I knew I never would.

It's strange how such a hard thing brought Ava and Zack closer together. I wish Ellie had someone like him. I wish she wasn't so alone.

I rub my eyes with the sleeve of my sweater, but it's scratchy and doesn't really wipe the tears away. I decide I should go back inside. I should be there when Ellie comes out. But as I make my way back to the door, Ellie and Liz are already coming out. Liz holds Ellie's hand as they step into the bright sun.

I walk up to them, but I don't know what to say, so I just walk behind them, back to the car.

Neither of them says a word all the way home. From the backseat, I watch the two of them, waiting for someone to say something. But Liz concentrates on the road and Ellie watches out the window. When Liz gets to my house, I feel awkward getting out of the car. I want to tell Ellie she'll be OK. I want to tell her she's my best friend. That she did the right thing. But I don't. I get out of the car and walk to our front door.

It isn't until Liz pulls out of our driveway that it hits me why it was over so fast.

Ellie didn't go through with it.

And if she didn't go through with it today, she probably never will.

I don't even think when I press the numbers. I just want to hear his voice.

"Hello?"

I can't say anything.

"Hello?" he says again.

"C-Caleb," I manage.

"Corinne? What's wrong?"

"I'm sorry," I say. My voice is shaky. "I'm sorry I got mad at you."

"Corinne, what's wrong? Are you all right?"

I picture Ellie and Liz coming out of the clinic, their awkward silence in the car. "She didn't do it," I say.

He doesn't answer.

I bite my lips together with my teeth. Warm tears slide down my cheeks and neck.

"But what does it mean?" he finally asks.

"I — I think she's going to have the baby."

When I get to school on Monday, I find the word on her locker. I knew Kayla and Jessie were going to get back at me for kicking the bathroom door and making them spill their concoction and stain their clothes. I just never thought they'd take it out on Ellie.

But there it is, staring at me on her locker door just as I am about to slip a note inside telling her that I will stand by her no matter what. That she is my best friend.

I search the hall to see if Ellie is anywhere in sight. I spot her way at the end. She hasn't seen the door yet.

I put the note in my pocket and use my hands to cover the big, ugly letters scratched into the metal.

S L U T

People walk by staring at me like I'm nuts, standing here with my hands on a locker door. But I don't care. I'll stand here all day if I have to. I swear I will.

Ellie can't see this. Not now. Especially not now.

She just can't.

chapter 25
Ellie

I'M NOT THE SAME ME ANYMORE. I walk down the hallway
toward my locker feeling—different.

I sat with Liz and Corinne in that row of chairs with all those
other women and girls looking at me. Wondering what I was
there for. If I was in as much trouble as they were.

They looked at Liz, too. I bet they thought she was my
mom. She held my hand. She asked me if I was OK. I kept
nodding and nodding.

"Yes. Yes. I'm OK," I said. "Stop asking me."

I didn't want her to be like my mother. To cry and look worried. I didn't want her to fall apart and make me feel like my

life was over. I wanted her to be strong. I wanted going there to feel like any other doctor's appointment.

So when she put her arm around me and tried to hug me close while we waited in the tiny exam room, I pulled away. I couldn't handle anyone being nice to me. Not there. Not when I was about to do this thing. To spare everyone else the pain. To make it all go away.

Only I knew it wouldn't. I knew I couldn't ever make it go away.

And then the nurse came back and smiled at me. "Ready?"

Liz got up—too fast. Too fast. She pulled my hand, but I didn't get up. I didn't move.

Come on, her pull said. *Let's get this over with.*

But I still didn't move. I just sat there. I wasn't nodding anymore. I was looking straight ahead.

So when Liz asked, "Ready, honey?" I said no.

"But it's time."

"No." I said it louder.

Liz gently pulled my hand again, but I twisted it out of her grasp.

"No." I think I yelled it.

Liz exchanged a look with the nurse, who was watching me with sympathetic eyes. I shook my head. *Stop looking at me!*

The nurse came closer with her clipboard. "Sweetie? What do you want to do?"

"No," I said, even though I wasn't answering her question. I wanted to keep saying it. I wanted to *scream* it. For all the times I should have. For all the times I could only say it in my head. All the times I held it in so I wouldn't disappoint the boys who told me they *had* to have me. Held it in while hoping they wanted more. Hoping they wanted me. Hoping they would stay and hold me and still want me. Hoping they would love me.

"No," I said again. "No. I'm not doing it." I tasted salt before I knew I was crying.

Liz pulled me to her and made some apologetic gesture to the nurse. We walked out.

In the hallway, I felt Liz's arms fold around me, holding me to her. This time I let her.

When we got in the elevator, Liz wiped my face with a pink tissue. I didn't look at her.

"We can go back," she said. "We can give it a week and try again."

"No."

"Are you sure, hon? Have you thought about what it would mean to keep it? A baby changes everything."

It's what my mother would say.

"For the rest of your life."

I watched our smudgy reflections in the metal elevator doors. "No," I said to them. Even though I knew it meant I was going to have to face my mother again. Even though I knew she would cry and look at me like my life was over. Like *her* life was over.

No.

Even though I would have to tell my father, too. And Luke.

No.

Even though I would have to face everyone at school.

No.

"No."

"OK, honey. All right. If that's what you want."

Liz put her warm hand around my waist and squeezed. "It'll be OK."

As I walk to my locker now, I feel that squeeze. I remember how, when she dropped me off, she took both my hands in hers and said the words again to my face. "You'll be OK." Like she really believed it. Even though she thought I was making the biggest mistake of my life.

Up ahead, Corinne is standing at my locker. Her hands are spread over part of the door.

"Hi." She looks nervous.

"What are you doing?"

"Let's go to class."

"But I need my books."

"Ellie."

"Move your hands," I say.

"Let's just go to class."

I reach for her skinny fingers. She tries to hold them there, but I pull them away.

The letters are big and thin. It looks like someone used a knife to scratch them there. People move by us and look. Some make that snickering noise people do when someone trips or has something on their face after lunch.

My hand automatically reaches for my stomach.

Corinne's hands move over my shoulders. "Are you OK?"

I want to say yes, but nothing comes out.

"Ellie, let's get out of here. We'll tell a teacher and have it fixed."

"Who did this?"

"It was probably those jerks Kayla and Jessie, El. They just did it to get back at us for that day in the bathroom, I bet."

But as I stare at the word, I realize it describes what I've felt like ever since that first time I was left alone after I went farthest. Like the bad girl I was never supposed to be.

A slut.

Corinne's fingers lace into mine and squeeze. "They're idiots. You know it's not true. Come on, let's go."

She pulls on my hand, but I untangle my fingers from hers.

"No." I open the door, get the books I need, and close it. When I do, the word stares back at me again.

SLUT

You are a slut.

I turn and walk away, feeling . . . different.

part three

MARCH

chapter 26

Ellie

EVERY MORNING THE KNIFE-THIN LETTERS greet me at
my locker. Corinne told me to complain. But what does it
matter? Getting rid of the word won't make this feeling
disappear.

I am a *S L U T.*

Sometimes I touch the letters, as if they might scratch my
fingers and make me bleed. Sometimes I hope they will.

I had to meet with the school counselor. Ms. Lyons. She
said I should consider homeschooling until after I have the
baby and things blow over. Like what's happening to me is
some kind of storm.

"You're putting me in a very awkward position," she
said. "On the one hand, you've set a good example, taking

responsibility for your bad choice. But I don't want you giving the other girls any ideas." She eyed my bulging stomach.

I wanted to ask her what she meant by my bad choice. Having sex? Or not having an abortion? Even though I know the answer.

"Or you could go to night school," she finally suggested. "Then come back in September and start out fresh."

How do I start out fresh? People don't forget.

Every day they watch me. They're measuring how my stomach grows. They elbow each other and whisper behind their hands. They do everything but point at my belly—the proof. I am what my locker says. I wear my sex on my stomach. I'm just like Hester in *The Scarlet Letter*. I can't go anywhere without looks. Without raised eyebrows. Without hearing their comments about me, as if I am the only highschooler in this town who ever got pregnant.

Think she's pregnant, or just fat? Bet her mother's proud. Hasn't she ever heard of birth control? She probably doesn't even know who the father is. Girls like that love to flaunt it. What a SLUT.

I try to avoid the places where I can hear those voices. The cafeteria. The grocery store. The sidewalk. The bus.

I stay in my room or go to Liz's, where it's safe. Where they don't talk about me and what I am or what I've done. Where they don't stare.

I stare, though. I look at myself sideways in the mirror and watch how I stick out. I try on all my baggiest clothes to try to hide what I wish was a secret. But none of them work.

I think the teachers are mad at me. Just like Ms. Lyons. They think I'm going to make other girls want to have babies. Like I want to do this. Like I wouldn't change things if I could. Like I look so happy.

I know Corinne thinks I made a big mistake. It would have been so much better, so much easier, if I'd gone with the original plan and gotten rid of the baby before it was . . . a real baby. She thinks that even if I give the baby away, I will always wonder where it is. I will always be filled with regret.

Maybe.

Some days I imagine keeping the baby. I would keep it quiet in my room, where no one else could see it. Or touch it. Or hurt it with their words. I pretend we could stay in there forever. Or we could hide in my little house in the backyard with Ginger and Cocoa.

Other days I pretend I'm not having a baby.

Last week I dreamed I had a kitten. When it came out, it mewed and licked me.

I held the little ball of fur in my hand and petted her. I asked my mother if I could keep her, but she said no.

"Cats are too much work. You have to clean their litter boxes. It will smell up the house. You have to give it away."

I started crying. I held the kitten to my face. She was warm and purring, and her nose was wet.

"Please let me keep her," I sobbed. "I love her. She needs me."

"Don't be silly. It's just a cat. Now, give it to me and I'll get rid of it for you." She pulled the kitten out of my hands and left me there.

The spot on my chest where the warm ball of fur had been turned cold. When I woke up, I felt kicking. I thought, for just a second, that it was the kitten.

Corinne is coming over soon. We're going to a Salvation Army store to find some baggy clothes. My mom would be upset if she found out. She thinks those places are dirty. That they smell. She's afraid of the people who work there.

Corinne thinks it's ironic that my mother is afraid.

"It's the *Salvation* Army," Corinne tells me when I explain our going has to be a secret. "How can she be afraid of people who want to save her?"

I don't tell her I know how it feels when everyone wants to

save you. How their wanting to save you makes you feel like you're going to die.

My mother cries so much now. Not in front of me, but I know. Her eyes are red and raw. I wish she would just be mad at me instead.

When I came back from the clinic and told her I changed my mind, she didn't say one word to me. She went to her room and shut the door. But I heard her sobbing on the other side. I put my hand on the door and told her through the keyhole that I was sorry.

I asked her to let me in, but she wouldn't answer.

When my father came home, I told him.

"*What?*" he asked. "Wh-why?"

"I couldn't." I choked the words out. "I just couldn't. I don't know."

"But—" Little prickles of sweat were forming on his forehead. I couldn't look at him. "Mom told me you had made up your mind. That you were—"

He couldn't even seem to say the words for the thing he wanted me to do to make it all go away.

"I'll give the baby up for adoption," I said. The words stung my throat.

"Honey. We should talk about this. It's not too late to change your mind and go back. Mom could take you."

"No," I said, trying to meet his eyes. "I'm not going back."

"Oh, God, Ellie." He stepped closer and put his hands on my shoulders. I don't know why, but I flinched. Just a little. It had been so long since he'd touched me.

He moved back.

If I had stayed still, would he have hugged me? Would he have held me and let me cry in his arms and told me everything would be OK?

Would he tell me he loved me?

But I flinched.

We looked at each other, not saying anything. I listened to our breath, his fast and panicked, mine slow and scared.

I'm sorry. I'm so sorry. I said it over and over in my head. But the words wouldn't come out again.

"Did you tell Mom?" he finally asked.

I nodded. "She's in the bedroom."

He looked away. Then he nodded, too.

"Shit."

"I won't keep the baby," I said again. "I don't want to keep the baby."

But as I cried the words, my hand moved to my stomach.

"Of course not. Right. Jesus Christ." He stepped away from me and made himself a drink, then one for my mother. He brought the drinks to their room and closed the door again. I didn't try to make them let me in.

I stood by myself, repeating those words in my head to make them be more true.

I don't want to keep the baby. I don't want to keep the baby. I don't want to keep . . .

That was three months ago. I still can't say the words out loud again. And it feels like my parents are still behind that door.

chapter 27

Caleb

ELLIE AND CORINNE sit on the couch with my mom and listen to her rant about civil rights, pretending Ellie isn't pregnant and that the whole school isn't talking about it. The three of them laugh at a private joke as if I don't exist. It's because I'm a guy. And all guys are scum now.

I decide to take my homework upstairs. When I get up from my usual spot on the floor, Corinne looks at me but doesn't ask where I'm going. I climb the stairs slowly, in case one of them wants to call me back, but no one does.

My room is freezing. I pull the down comforter off my bed and wrap it around me while I sit at my desk and try to focus on my trig homework. Their laughing echoes up the stairs and makes it impossible to concentrate. Without thinking, I reach for the phone and call Josh.

As soon as the phone rings, I regret it, but he answers before I can hang up.

"Hey, it's me," I say.

"What's up?" he asks, as if it hasn't been, like, two weeks since we've hung out.

"Not much. Trig."

"Yeah, me too. Sucks. Wanna take a break?"

"What'd you have in mind?" I ask.

"The usual, I guess."

"Is Dave with you?"

"Nah, he's too busy with his new girlfriend. *Evette.*"

"Isn't she a senior?"

"Yeah, he thinks he's a stud now."

"That's all we need."

"I'll grab a few from my old man and come get you."

"No," I say, a little too fast. All I need is him showing up at the door with Ellie and Corinne sitting there. "I'll be there in ten."

I go downstairs and stop in the living room. "I'm going out," I say.

My mom doesn't ask me who with because she knows the answer. She gives me a *You be careful* look, and I give her my look that says *Whatever.* Corinne gives me a *I know you're going to see that asshole* glare.

Ellie is the only one who says "Bye" out loud.

I shut the door behind me and walk into the freeze. My car still isn't warmed up when I get to Josh's house. He steps out as soon as I pull into the driveway. His jacket is all puffed up with beer cans. He glances back at the house nervously a few times before he gets into the car.

He pulls out a can and hands it to me.

"Thanks. Where to?"

He shrugs and reaches inside his coat for another beer, which he opens and chugs. I take us a few blocks away where a new development is going in. There's a portable toilet with a huge padlock on it, and one of those mobile homes the contractors use for an office. My car's headlights shine out over a group of empty lots. Some have foundations half-dug but left until the ground thaws. They look like a bunch of giant, open graves.

I cut the lights in case any cops are cruising the area, but leave the key in so we can blast the heat and music. We drink and listen for a while. Josh finishes his beer and unrolls the window to throw the can.

"Put it on the floor," I say. "I'll take care of it."

He gives me a surprised look and instead of throwing the

can out, shakes it so the last drips fall onto the ground outside before he tosses the can on the floor, like that's what he
planned to do all along. He cracks open another and takes a
long drink, then leans back into his seat.

"So, have you talked to her lately?" he asks. He never says
her name.

"Not really," I tell him. "She doesn't talk to me much. Just
to my mom and Corinne."

"Is she, you know, OK?"

He won't face me when he asks.

I shake my head. "She seems to be, I guess."

Sometimes, after Corinne and Ellie leave the house, my
mom tells me stuff she notices about the baby. Like that the
baby's kicking now. But when Ellie's over, no one says a word
about what's happening.

Corinne told me that Ellie's plan is to give the baby up for
adoption. But my mom said only like one percent of mothers
actually go through with it. The ones who do must go crazy
not knowing where the baby is or if it's happy and stuff. My
own dad at least knows where I am if he ever *does* decide to
see me again. He was my mom's best friend, and when she
decided she wanted to have a baby, he donated his sperm. I
guess I get the not knowing thing a little, since I have a half
brother and sister I've never met. Still, when it's your own

baby—I don't know. I'm sure it's a million times worse. I mean, if Ellie decides not to keep the baby, I bet every time she even sees a baby, she'll wonder if it's hers. And as the baby grows up, she'll know how old it would be, and she'll see little kids and wonder if one of them is hers. At least, I would. I wonder if Josh will, too.

Josh sighs and finishes his beer. I've never seen him drink this fast.

"I saw what happened to her locker."

He's watching out the window again, so I can't see his face. He holds his beer sort of resting on his left thigh. His hand is shaking.

"It sucks, you know? Just because you get pregnant doesn't mean you screwed around with everyone. So she did it with a few guys. So what?"

I take a long drink of what's left of my own beer, which is flat and warm now. I don't know what to say. It's not like his stupid strutting around in the locker room helped her case any.

"Everything is just so fucked up," he says. "I'm going to be a father—but not a father—at the same time. And Ellie's walking around with—" He chokes up but covers it by taking another drink. "It's just so fucked up."

I nod and watch the darkness out my window. "Yeah," I tell him. "It is."

We don't look at each other again. We stare out our own windows. I don't know how much time goes by. I can tell he's crying, because I hear the sniffs. I turn up the music so he doesn't have to worry about me hearing—and I don't have to listen.

As the music blasts between us, I wonder if my dad ever cried about leaving me. If he ever wonders how I'm doing, beyond the yearly updates my mom sends him on my birthday. I wonder if he ever thinks of me beyond that one day a year my mom forces him to remember.

I'm pretty sure I know the answer.

chapter 28

Josh

"WHERE'VE YOU BEEN?"

He's waiting by the door in the dark of the living room. His breath tells me he's had his usual six-pack. The TV light casts a glow over his face as a scene changes on the screen. He looks like the guy from *The Shining,* but I'm smart enough not to tell him that.

I try to step back a little. Whatever I say is going to piss him off, so I don't answer. It's only a matter of time before he starts the lecture. I can hear it already. *You keep it up and you'll end up a sorry-ass loser like me. Is that what you want?*

No, Dad.

My head is spinning and I can hardly stand up, and I really just want to go to bed and pass out. But here it comes . . .

"You think I don't notice when you take beer from the fridge?"

The damn dog is standing next to him, breathing at me. "Hey, Rosie girl," I say, hoping that if I'm nice to her he won't notice I'm ignoring his question.

"You going to answer me or what?"

Guess not.

"Sorry, Dad." Shit. What was the first question? I'm totally buzzed, and maybe that will be a good thing if he's going to start telling me what a screwup I'm turning into.

"Uh, I was with Caleb. Hanging out."

"Yuh. Hanging out with a twelve-pack."

"Well, yeah. I borrowed a few. I'll pay you back."

"You think that's what I care about right now?" He rubs his hand on his chin that way he does when he's thinking. His rough hand drags across his stubble, making a quiet scraping noise.

"Come over here." He flicks the floor lamp on next to the couch and sits down. Jesus, he looks like shit. He's still wearing his work shirt, all grease-stained, with his company name embroidered on the pocket: HAL'S DETAIL. Dave always jokes about what his "detail" has to do with anything. Ever since the third grade, Dave has been able to make any word sound dirty.

My dad thumps the space on the couch next to him with his big hand. For the first time since I can remember, I sit beside him. I try not to smell all the smells coming off him. The stale alcohol, the grease, the hamburger he ate for dinner.

"I've been talking to Mikey."

"Yeah?" I'm a little relieved. His conversations with Mike focus on washed-up 90s bands, football, beer, and who had the cooler car in high school.

"Yeah," he says, all serious.

"What?"

"He told me you got yourself into some trouble with a girl."

Oh, shit.

I lean way back into the couch and take a deep breath.

He shifts next to me and shakes his head.

"So it's true." He leans closer to me and looks at me like I'm the biggest idiot in the world. "Damn it, Josh! I thought you knew better. Didn't I tell you to always wear a condom no matter what?"

"I did, Dad. I swear! But I think it fell off while I was—you know. I don't know how it happened. I *was* trying to be careful!"

He looks me in the eye for a minute. I stare back so he sees

I'm telling the truth. The whites of his eyes are bloodshot. He looks like he hasn't slept in days. I blink my own eyes and wonder if they look the same.

How the hell did he end up such a pitiful mess? Doesn't my mom notice what's happening? I mean, she's a nurse, for Christ's sake. Doesn't she care that her family is a fucking wreck?

I press my head against the back of the couch and try to hold down the need to puke.

"Look, bud. This is serious shit."

Like I don't know that.

He shifts on the couch again. The man suddenly can't get comfortable on the thing he spends half his life on.

"Just be glad the girl's taking care of things without involving you. At least that's what Mike heard. Is it true?"

I nod.

"Good. Take it from me: a kid's the last thing you need in your life at your age." He reaches for his beer on the coffee table. He takes a long drink before he puts the can down again.

As I listen to him swallow, I think about what he just said.

"What do you mean, *take it from you?*" I ask.

"Huh? Oh, nothing."

"No, not nothing. You said it like it happened to you."

He picks up his can again and drinks in long, slow gulps.

"What did you mean, Dad? Did this happen to you, too?"

He lowers his beer and rests it on his belly so he can look inside it. Like there's some answer in there that will save him from my question. "Not exactly like this."

But I've already figured it out.

I'm the answer.

I'm the reason my mom married my father.

I knew my parents were really young when they got married, but I thought it was because they were in love. Not because they had to. Not because of me.

"That makes sense," I say. "That's just perfect. The only reason you and Mom got married is because of me. I was a fuckup from the day I was born."

"Watch your language," he says. "And don't you believe that for a second."

He puts his beer back down and rubs his hands on his thighs. "Your mother loved me. Don't ask me why, but the crazy girl actually *wanted* to marry me. You were just a good excuse."

Loved. Past tense. But he smiles at the memory.

"Back then I was working in a regular band, a *real* band,

and your mom'd come to all our sets. Never missed a show. But—" He trails off.

"What?"

"Eh. Life happens. I needed a steadier job to support you two." He tips his head back and closes his eyes.

"So you gave up your dream because of *me*?"

"No, Joshy," he says, sitting up. He puts his large oven mitt of a hand on my thigh and squeezes in a firm way. It feels so weird to have him touch me. Like this. Like he's hanging on to me. "No. You never believe that, you hear me? Sometimes you have to set priorities. You and your mom were more important to me than being some B-list rocker. Let's face it. I was never gonna be the next Eric Clapton."

"But you'll never know now. And it's all my fault!"

"Don't be stupid. What, it's your fault you were born? Last time I checked, I don't think you had much choice in the matter."

I press my lips together and force myself not to lose it in front of my old man. He can say whatever he wants, but I'll always be the reason his dreams didn't come true. Maybe the reason he and my mom are so miserable.

"Josh," he says, squeezing my leg even tighter. "You listen to me. Don't go down that road. I can tell you're sitting there blaming yourself for something you had no control over. Look at me. I wouldn't change how things happened. You understand?"

I can't look at him. "OK, Dad," I say.

"I'll break the news to your mom," he says quietly. "Better she hears it from me than one of her gossipy friends at work."

I nod. Figures the one thing that gets them to say two words to each other is my colossal screwup.

"Now go sleep it off, son. That's not gonna feel good in the morning."

He takes his hand away and leans back into the couch. As big as he is, the couch seems to swallow him. My thigh feels cold where his hand was, and I wish he'd grab hold again.

When I get to my room, I shut the door and lean against it, staring into the dark. The room spins around me. I make it to my bed and try to hold on until the spins wear off. As my eyes adjust to the dark, I watch my desk seem to rise up in front of me over and over again. I shut my eyes, but then I feel like I'm going to fall off the bed.

Shit.

Shit!

This is it.

This is my life.

I should have known. All one big fucking mistake.

I picture my mom helping me ride my bike when I was little. That way she smiled at me. Was that a fake? Was she pretending so she could hide the truth about how miserable she was, trapped in this crappy marriage all because of me? Or did she really love my dad once, like he said?

There's a photo album with my baby pictures in it. Pictures of me with my mom holding me. Playing with me. She was always smiling. Not those fake smile-for-the-camera smiles, but smiling *at me*. I never wondered before who took those pictures, but it must have been my dad. He must have seen her being happy through that little window in the camera.

I can't remember many pictures of my dad. Just a few from parties with him in the background, a beer can in his hand, of course. And the one of him playing his guitar for me in the living room. I was standing in a playpen with pajamas on, listening. I used to stare at the photo all the time and try to remember what the music sounded like, but I never managed to. It was probably the last time he ever played for me.

I close my eyes again and fight the spinning. But even with my eyes closed, I feel the room turning and twisting in the dark.

*   *   *

I wake up to someone knocking on my door. The clock next to my bed says 1:24 a.m.

"Josh?" The door creaks open quietly. My mom peeks her head in. The light from the hall shines in my eyes.

"Hey," I say. As I wake up, I feel a headache settle into my brain and pound on my skull. My eyes feel like they're going to explode out of my head.

"Sorry to wake you, honey. I had a long night and—I wanted to check in with you. We keep missing each other, seems like."

She steps into my dark room.

I pull myself up on my elbow. Her face is splotchy, the way it gets when she cries.

"Dad told you, didn't he?"

She nods.

I let my head fall back onto my pillow.

"Oh, Josh."

I wish I knew what to say.

"Honey." She puts her hand on my arm. I'm sure I smell like stale beer. Like my dad. I try to hold in my breath and breathe into my chest.

"I'm sorry," I say. "I—" But what else is there?

"I know, honey," she says. She leans forward and kisses my forehead. She hasn't done that in so long. She's still wearing her nurse's uniform. She smells like old people and disinfectant. I can't even remember the last time we had more than a one-minute conversation with me running late for school or her rushing off to work or the soup kitchen or anywhere else but here. This is one hell of a way to reunite.

"Get some sleep," she says. "We can talk more in the morning. Or—whenever you want. I'm here."

She pauses before she leaves, standing in the bright doorway. Her face looks so tired and worn-out. "You'll get through this, Josh."

"I know," I lie.

She steps back into the hall and closes my door. I listen to the floor creak under her feet as she makes her way down the hall. I wait to hear their bedroom door close before I roll over and cry like a baby.

chapter 29

Corinne

I'M IN THE GIRLS' BATHROOM hiding out from Kayla and Jessie again. We're officially at war. After they did the *SLUT* thing to Ellie, I tried to *BITCH* them back. Unfortunately I only got up to the *T* on Kayla's locker before they caught me. They've been harassing me ever since. I could report them, but then I'd have to fess up about my part in this whole thing, and I really don't think being forced into mediation with those two would change anything.

Of course, sitting here crouched with my feet on the toilet seat isn't exactly my idea of fun, either. The truth is, I've been doing a lot of thinking during these hideout sessions. Mostly about Ellie. Like why she refuses to report the locker thing. Sometimes I think she believes she deserves to be labeled a slut. Sometimes, I think Ellie believes that getting pregnant is her punishment. And that just drives me crazy.

The other night when I was sitting next to her at Liz's, she jumped a little and put her hand on her belly. The baby must have been kicking or whatever they do. It must be weird to feel something living inside you.

Whenever Ava or I have a birthday, my mom and dad get out our photo album and show us pictures of my mom when she was pregnant. My dad took a picture of her every month so we could see how we grew inside her. The two of them always get misty-eyed and embarrassingly affectionate when they gush over the photos. I wish Ellie could enjoy pregnancy like that. It must be awful to have this little person living in you, that you'll never know. That you spend all day trying to pretend isn't even there. That you try to hide.

When the late bell rings, I listen hard for footsteps before I step down from the toilet seat. As soon as I'm sure it's all clear, I sprint out of the bathroom and down the hall to homeroom. As I rush past Ellie's locker, I punch the word with my fist.

"Hey! What did that locker ever do to you?" I almost trip at the sound of Caleb's voice behind me.

I rub my hand. "It's my new thing. It makes me feel better."

"Really?" He walks over to Ellie's locker and gives it a good punch, then shakes his fist like he broke his hand.

"Um. I don't feel better." When he looks at me, my stomach melts.

I guess I didn't realize how long it's been since I actually laughed, because my mouth feels strange when I do, as if it forgot how. It's been forever since I've really talked to Caleb, and it feels good to be with him again, just us.

"We're gonna be so late," I say.

He grins mischievously. "Wanna ditch?"

"You mean leave? Now?"

"Yeah. Let's do it." His eyes sparkle.

"OK," I say.

"Where to?"

I scan the hallway and don't see anyone. "Let's just get out of here and then decide."

We hurry down the hall and outside into the parking lot. A few late students are rushing into the building, but no teachers.

Caleb unlocks the car door on my side to let me in. It's the first time anyone has done that for me.

"So, where do you wanna go?" he asks when he climbs in.

An image of the two of us fooling around in my room comes to mind.

Hmmmm.

No.

Erase image.

Ever since that day Ellie came out of the clinic, the whole idea of getting close to someone and then having sex scares the hell out of me. I guess Ellie finally did it. She cured me of my sex drive.

Maybe.

"I don't know," I say. "It's kind of nice out. Somewhere outside?"

"I know the perfect place," he says.

I lean back in my seat and enjoy what seems like my very first date. We drive away from the school and down the main road that leads out of town. Within a few minutes, I know exactly where we're going.

When we get to the park, we head straight for the seesaw.

We spend the whole morning hanging out on the playground. It's pretty cold, but not so bad for March. After we try out every piece of playground equipment at least three times, we decide to take a rest. We go over to the merry-go-round and lie down with our legs bent over the side so we can make ourselves turn with our feet. The metal is warm from the sun. I close my eyes as we glide in circles.

"Do you ever wish you were a little kid again?" Caleb asks.

I turn my head and squint to see him. His eyes are closed, and the sun on his face gives it a warm glow. Liz really nailed it when she painted him as a cherub.

"Sometimes," I say, thinking about what things were like before everything changed with Ellie. "Maybe more lately."

"Me, too. Only I imagine having a different childhood."

"*You?* But Liz is amazing! It must have been cool to grow up with her. I bet she let you break all the rules."

"Seriously?" He opens his eyes to look at me. "Don't you ever get tired of her 'I'm such a hip mom' act?"

"I don't think it's an act. I think she's great. I mean, look how much she's helped Ellie. Your mom is smart. And *fun*. I think you're lucky!"

He closes his eyes again and doesn't say anything for a while, but the silence isn't the awkward kind.

"You know that painting in the living room?" he asks. "The one of the man?"

"With the eyes?"

"Yeah. He's . . . um . . . my dad. He left when I was, like, one."

"Wow."

"He and my mom were best friends, and my mom wanted a baby so she asked him and . . ." He sighs. "My mom kind of figured he'd stick around, you know? But he met someone and they moved to the West Coast and had their own kids. I guess I didn't really count."

"Wow," I say again. "You mean, he doesn't keep in touch?"

"Not really. He visited a few times when I was little, but after a while he stopped. It's not a big deal, I guess. It's not like he wanted to have a family with my mom. She promised him all she wanted from him was, you know, his sperm."

"But you think she wanted more?"

We turn in silence for a while as he thinks. "Yeah. I think she expected more."

"Do you wish he stayed?"

"I used to. I used to go to the park and see other little kids with their mom and dad and wish I had a dad like they did. Liz never taught me how to play baseball or any 'guy' stuff. She said it was all gender bias. When I turned five, she gave me a dollhouse for my birthday when I'd asked for a Transformer. I used to get so mad at her. It's funny, looking back on it now."

"You really liked that dollhouse, I bet."

"I'm not the only one."

"Ooh, tell me Josh and Dave liked it, too!"

He laughs and lifts his face to the sun. "I'll never tell."

"I knew it!" I say, laughing too.

He reaches for my hand. "Thanks," he says. When we touch, my stomach drops as if I'm on the swings.

"For what?"

"Making me laugh. It's been a while." His fingers lace through mine and squeeze. His hand isn't warm or cold; it's the same temperature as mine. I squeeze back and keep holding on. I feel scared and safe.

He moves closer to me. His hand is still clasped with mine. I keep holding on and so does he. I shut my eyes and wait. He moves even closer, then kisses me on the cheek. His warm lips barely brush against my skin.

When he moves his head back to where it was, I feel where his lips touched my cheek and know I want more.

I move my face closer to his.

"Again," I say quietly. Under normal circumstances I would probably die of embarrassment for letting those words escape. But Caleb leans toward me again and aims for my cheek. Without thinking, I turn my head and close my eyes and pray my lips meet his lips and not his nose or eyebrow.

Our lips touch, then press against each other, then open,

just slightly. His soft, wet tongue gently finds its way to mine and we're actually kissing and my whole body is on fire. I don't dare open my eyes. I just let his hand reach up around me and hold my chin while we kiss and spin, so slowly, like in a dream. He smells and tastes like cold, fresh air.

I take him all in and repeat to myself that this isn't a dream; this is a perfect moment. This is the perfect first kiss I've been waiting for all my life.

chapter 30

Ellie

I'M SUPPOSED TO BE DOING MY HOMEWORK, but the baby won't stop moving. I get up from my desk and lie down on my bed. I know I shouldn't do this. I shouldn't try to feel. But I can't help it.

I slip my shirt up over my belly. I put both hands on it and press. It feels like the baby is pressing back, trying to get out. Or maybe just exploring its tiny home. It doesn't know that all it will ever know of me is the inside.

I stretch my fingers across my belly and glide my hand back and forth, waving softly. Sometimes I think I feel a hand reaching out for mine. Or it could be a foot, kicking my hand away. I wish I could tell the difference.

Whenever I feel movement, I reach down to feel whatever

is poking out. I've seen Liz watch me. Our eyes meet and she winks, but she never says anything. I think she knows it would hurt too much if we started talking about it. If we started to love it. So I just lie here and feel these shapes and try to guess what they are.

My bedroom door opens, and my mother steps in and jumps at the sight of me.

"Oh." She's holding a laundry basket full of my brother's dirty clothes. She looks away quickly.

"Sorry. I didn't know you were in here." She says it like I'm a stranger, not her daughter.

I pull down my shirt fast. But I know she saw by the way she jerked her head away. She saw my round belly and my belly button sticking out. She saw my baby.

She rushes over to my hamper and adds my dirty clothes to the rest. I sit up, holding my shirt over my belly.

"Mom?"

"I'm sorry," she says again. Her voice is shaky. "I didn't know you were in here." She says it to the window looking out over our front yard, though. Not to me.

I want to tell her I'm the one who is sorry. I want to tell her not to be so sad.

Her shoulders start to tremble, but she doesn't turn around. She just holds on to that basket of dirty laundry, facing the window, her fingers curled tightly around the handles.

She takes a deep breath. Maybe she will finally talk to me. Maybe she will finally let me tell her how things happened, if I dare.

But she turns to leave.

"Mom?" I say the word calmly. I don't want her to go. Suddenly, I want so badly to talk. I want her to be more than that orange-juice-commercial mom. I want her to stop doing the laundry and making breakfast. I want her to see inside me. I want her to hug me and hold me and tell me she would take the pain for me if she could. Just like she did when I was little and I hurt myself. I want her to fill me up with her words. I want her to say something. Anything. I want her to tell me it's all right. That everything is going to be OK. Even if we both know it's a lie.

"Mom, please don't go."

She finally turns toward me. Her cheeks have tear lines, and her nose is running.

I move to the edge of the bed. Closer to her. "I'm sorry, Mom." My own tears slide down my jaw and drip onto my shirt.

She sniffs and wipes her wet cheek on her shoulder. "I know, baby."

I put my feet on the floor and start to hoist myself up. But as I rise, she walks to the door.

"I'm sorry, too."

I step forward, but she's gone. I listen to her go down the stairs and start the wash.

I touch my belly again. It makes me feel so empty and full at the same time. I have to wonder, after the baby is born, how I'll ever fill the space.

part four

JUNE

chapter 31

Ellie

I'M LYING IN MY ROOM listening to the birds outside. I used to think they sang because they were happy. But then I learned on a nature show that they're really showing off. Trying to lure some other bird so they can mate with it. Or let the other birds know not to get too close to their turf. I wish I'd never seen that show. Because now all I think about is what those pretty sounds mean. And how they're not pretty at all.

Liz gave me some books. *Our Bodies, Ourselves* and *What to Expect When You're Expecting.* On the cover of the second one, a woman sits in a rocking chair. She's rocking the baby inside her. It's a strange picture for that book. Because even though it's a drawing, I don't think she looks happy. And I wonder what she's expecting. What am I?

I don't have a rocking chair, but sometimes I sit in my pink beanbag chair and hold my belly in my hands, listening to the beads settle underneath me like rain. I feel the baby quietly moving around to get comfortable. I feel shapes press against my hands, slowly, slowly, pushing against my palms and fingers, and I push back gently to say *Hello. I'm here.*

Whenever the baby stops moving, I wait, push my hands against my stomach, then shift a little until I feel the baby move under my fingers again. Just to make sure the baby is still OK.

At school I feel Josh watching me. He follows me, keeping his distance. I remember his hands on me, reaching to get inside. I don't know what he wants now. I don't know if he wants to talk to me. But I can't. I can't look at his hands. I can't hear his voice or smell his breath. I can't even look at his face.

I tried to read the books because Liz said to. She said I should do the exercises. She's worried. She knows it's going to hurt.

They say not to sleep on your back. Or sit in hot tubs. Or change your cat's litter box. They say to do weird exercises. Kegels. Pelvic tilt. Dromedary droop. They tell you to do all this stuff. So your back doesn't hurt. To keep you from tearing. To make sure your body recovers from childbirth.

I think of the movies and TV shows of women screaming while they give birth. Saying they hate men. Saying they will never have sex again. And crying. Because it hurts so much.

My heartbeat quickens and my forehead gets damp thinking about it. I have to squeeze my hands into fists and bite my knuckles so I don't scream out before I even feel any pain.

How am I going to do this?

When Luke knocks on my door, I forget about the birds and the pain. I stop thinking about the little hand or foot pushing against my insides.

"Time for school," he says. He avoids looking near my belly. They all do. "If you hurry, I'll take you." He turns and thuds down the carpeted stairs like he always does.

I hoist myself up and pull on the Salvation Army shirt I wear to cover my belly. I don't look in the mirror. I don't care. School will be over in three more weeks. Ms. Lyons will be so relieved when I'm finally gone. No more worrying about other girls wanting to have babies. No more worrying about the school's image.

No more me.

chapter 32

Josh

I'M OFFICIALLY A STALKER. When the last bell rings, I know
she'll come out of study hall and I wait at the end of the hallway, pretending to look for something in my locker. She
comes out of the room, looking at the floor while people hurry
by her. She walks slowly, as if her back hurts. As soon as she
heads toward the opposite end of the hall, I follow, keeping
my distance. When she gets near her locker, she turns and I
see her belly sticking out. My heart beats faster, like it always
does. I quickly step out of sight.

That's my baby.

Our baby.

She tries to hide the bump with baggy clothes—T-shirts with plaid button-up shirts over them that don't button at all. But I can see it.

That's my baby growing in there.

I've heard about girls who hid being pregnant all the way up until they had the baby. One girl had a baby in the bathroom during her prom or some crazy shit like that. But Ellie doesn't try that hard to cover it up. What's the point? Everyone knows. Still, she doesn't make a big show of it, either.

Sometimes people stop talking when they see me coming down the hall. I don't know why they bother. It's not like I don't know what they're saying. *There's the asshole who knocked her up. There's the idiot who couldn't figure out how to use a condom. What a loser.*

I'm sure they all speculate about what's going to happen after the baby is born. The truth is, they probably know more than I do.

Caleb says Ellie plans to give the baby up for adoption. I tell myself that's the best thing. To give the baby to someone who really wants it.

But what if I wanted it? Why don't I get a say?

Yeah.

I know that's crazy.

But so is the fact that there's going to be this kid out

there—*my kid*—and I'm never going to know it. I'll never know if it was a boy or a girl. I'll never find out if it looked like me. Or talked like me. Or felt about things the way I do.

I know if I wanted to, I could probably take some test and prove the baby's mine. Take custody. But what a joke. What baby would stand a chance living in my fucked-up house?

Crazy.

I guess that's why I keep following Ellie around, sneaking glimpses of our growing baby. Because that's all I'll ever get.

I guess that's why I feel like I'm sinking underwater and I can't breathe and I can't call out for help because there's no one there to pull me out anyway.

I guess that's why I feel like I'll die if I don't see my baby before it's gone for good.

chapter 33
Caleb

"PROMISE ME YOU'LL TELL ME WHEN IT HAPPENS."

Josh looks at me in this desperate way, like people do in movies when they've been shot through the chest and are trying to utter their last words. Don't ask me how I'll find out when Ellie goes into labor, but I nod and promise anyway.

"Do you think it will be soon?" Josh asks.

We're sitting in my room for a change. My mom has a Saturday morning class, and Josh said he needed an escape from his house but didn't feel like going to the park. He didn't bother to stop for Dave on his way here. Dave's always with his new girlfriend, anyway. And when he's not with her, he's telling us about their amazing sex life and every other little thing about her enough to drive us nuts.

I don't tell them about Corinne. We haven't told anyone about us, actually. I guess we both feel too guilty about being happy with everything that's happening.

"My mom thinks Ellie could have the baby any day now," I answer.

"Guess I better get going before she gets back," he says.

"My mom doesn't hate you," I tell him.

"Yeah, right."

"She knows you made a mistake. That's all."

He doesn't answer. I follow him down the stairs and into the entryway. Before he gets to the door, he sees the overnight bag my mom put by the door.

"Your mom going somewhere?" he asks.

"Uh . . . it's for Ellie," I say. "My mom put some stuff together for her, you know, for when she's in the hospital."

"Oh. Right." He stares at the bag, like he wants to know what's inside, but he doesn't ask.

For the past few weeks, my mom has been adding stuff to the bag. The jazz CD she plays when Ellie's here. The soft kind of tissues with lotion in them. A pair of slippers. Some magazines. I thought about putting the teakettle bird in there, too, just to let her know my mom wasn't the only one thinking about her. But in the end, I decided not to. I don't know why. Maybe I just don't want her thinking about saving things. Even metal birds.

When Josh opens the door to leave, my mom is running up the porch steps, out of breath.

"Oh! Hi." She looks at me for help, but I have no idea what to say.

"Josh, I haven't seen you in ages. Um . . ." She reaches for Ellie's bag. "It's time," she says awkwardly. "Stay by the phone, OK? I'll call you as soon as I know anything."

She starts to turn, then stops.

"Are you all right?" she asks Josh.

He opens his mouth but can't seem to answer. My mom gives him a hug. She's smaller than him, but he leans into her as tears start to run down his cheeks. I look away.

"I've got to go," my mom says finally, easing herself away from Josh. "Everything's going to be OK," she tells him.

He nods, wiping his face with the back of his forearm.

The screen door slams shut. Josh steps back and stumbles. I grab his arm to keep him up.

"I'm going," he tells me.

Crap. I put my hand on the door to stop him. "Josh, I don't think that's a good idea."

He puts his own hand on the door. "Why not?"

"Because. I don't think—I'm not sure Ellie—"

"Don't worry. I know she doesn't want to see me. She won't even know I'm there. It's my kid, too, Cay. Or did you forget?"

"I didn't forget. I just—" A warm breeze drifts in the door. It smells like cut grass. It reminds me of the park and going there with Josh and Dave when we were little.

"I have to try to see the baby, OK? I can't explain why." His voice cracks. "I just want to see before they take my baby away. That's all." He's shaking.

I'm surprised by the pain I feel in my own chest. I don't know why I feel this way when the baby isn't even mine, but I do. I feel . . . helpless.

"OK," I say. "I'll come with you."

"No, Cay. You stay here. This is something I have to do on my own."

He takes off out the door. From the window, I watch him run down the driveway and continue along the road. It's not until I figure out he's going to run all the way to the hospital that I realize I should have told him to take my car. And that it didn't even occur to him that he could have asked.

chapter 34

Corinne

"How's she doing?" Liz asks.

My cell is sweaty from my palm. I didn't know my palms could sweat this much. I look over at Ellie, who is sitting in the passenger seat of my mom's car. Her face is red as she concentrates on breathing. "OK," I say.

"How far apart are the contractions?"

"Still five or six minutes."

"All right. That's good. You're on your way, right?"

"Yes," I say. "We're about ten minutes away. We already called Ellie's parents, and they're going to meet us there."

"Good. Just tell her to try to stay as relaxed as possible. And keep telling her she's doing great."

"I will."

I hang up and reach for Ellie's hand. "Liz says to try to stay relaxed."

She breathes in and out slowly, nodding. "I need you to pull over."

"But—"

"Please. I'm just—I'm not ready yet."

I do what she says and pull over at the first place we come to, which is a McDonald's parking lot. The smell of French fries wafts inside the car.

"Uh . . ." Ellie holds her side and leans forward.

I reach over and put my hand on her knee. "Try to take slow breaths," I say, trying to sound as calm as possible.

"I'm scared," she says to the windshield.

Me, too.

"I know," I say. "But we should probably get going."

"Just give me a minute. I just need—some time."

We watch people come out of the restaurant. People in suits rushing in during their breaks, too impatient for the drive-through. Moms clutching their kids' hands as they pull ahead, whining for their Happy Meals.

Ellie puts her hands under her belly again and closes her eyes.

I check the clock and try to figure out how long we have until the next contraction. Liz thought Ellie should take birthing classes, but Ellie refused. She couldn't bear to be around all those happy couples. She read every book she and Liz could find, but I think the more she read, the more afraid she got.

I wait for the digital clock to mark another minute. Then another. Then Ellie pitches forward and moans. Her face is beet red. Her forehead is wet with sweat, even though the AC is making it feel like the Arctic in here.

"OK," she says when the contraction finally passes. "I guess it's time." The last words sound like they hurt to say.

I nod, put the car in reverse, and stall. My hands are shaking. I fumble with the keys and restart the car.

Ellie looks straight ahead and continues breathing.

I pull out of the parking lot without even looking.

Tires squeal behind me, and a guy in a pickup truck gives me the finger.

"Same to you!" I yell, flipping him back.

Ellie leans forward. "It hurts," she says quietly. "It hurts so much."

"We're almost there," I tell her.

Ellie writhes in the seat next to me.

"You can cry, Ellie," I say. "You can scream if you want. You don't have to be brave." But she just grits her teeth as my own tears start to run down my cheeks.

The drive seems endless, but we finally arrive and I pull into the emergency entrance, jump out, and run around the car for Ellie. Her eyes plead with me through the window. I wish I could take her away from all this, go back in time and let her do it all differently. But all I can do is smile weakly at her and open the door. As I help Ellie out of the car, Liz pulls into the parking lot. When Ellie sees her, she finally starts to cry. Liz hugs her tight. Then Ellie's parents show up and everyone crowds around Ellie so that they sort of swallow her up. I get pushed aside as they escort her across the parking lot.

I don't even get to say good-bye to her. Or tell her good luck. I want to hug her and tell her I'm here and that I'm so sorry for everything. That I'm sorry for not understanding why she was with those guys. And for not understanding why she decided to have the baby. For thinking she was crazy. Even stupid. I want to tell her I'm sorry for not covering up the word on her locker just because she asked me not to.

I don't get to tell her I think she's amazing for surviving all this crap in the first place. Or that someone *will* love her.

I don't get to tell her that *I* love her.

I don't get to do anything but watch them take her away.

I follow behind as they make their way quickly through those sliding doors, then another set of solid ones I'm not allowed to go through.

I stand in the hallway until someone comes over and tells me I need to move my car. I go out and park where I'm supposed to, then head back to the hospital. My feet feel heavy as I walk. When I get inside, I go straight to the desk and they tell me to follow the pink lines on the wall that say maternity. The hallways all have these color-coded lines on them for people to follow. Every time I turn a corner, I read the word *maternity* on the pink line. I hope Ellie didn't notice it. It seems too cheerful.

I ask at the nurses' station what's happening, but the woman working behind the desk says she doesn't know and I'll have to wait. Her phone rings, and she turns her back to me.

I realize I left my cell in the car so I find a pay phone near the waiting room and call Caleb collect. He picks up on the first ring.

"Hello?" he says after accepting the charges.

"We're at the hospital," I say.

"Is everything OK?"

"I don't know." My hands are shaking. "I think so."

"Are—are you OK?" His voice cracks.

"I'm not sure."

"I'm on my way. I'll be right there."

The phone clicks, but I don't hang up. I let the buzz hum

in my ear. Some people walk by me. I turn into the phone box so I can cry. Just hold the phone and cry with that steady buzz in my ear. I wonder how many people have cried into this same mouthpiece. How many have called to say "It's a boy!" or "It's a girl!"? How many have called to say "It's over"?

How many have stood here and listened to the phone buzz, not moving. Just standing still and wondering how to move forward. How to move at all.

A man taps me on the shoulder and motions for the phone. He looks like a grandfather. He has tears in his eyes, but he's got a huge grin on his face.

I wipe my own face and step aside.

I find a chair with empty ones on either side and sit down. There are other people in the room. I try not to look at them. Instead I stare at the dusty-blue rug and wait for Caleb.

I feel him before I see him. His hand gently touches my shoulder. I was thinking about Ellie. Dreaming almost. About when we were little and we put on my sister's old dresses and had tea parties with our stuffed animals. Ellie taught me to hold my pinkie out when I took a sip, and we talked with British accents about the weather and how tasty our cookies were.

Caleb touches my cheek and turns my face toward him.

"You all right?"

I nod, but at the sound of his voice I start to cry again.

He sits next to me so I can lean into him. He wraps his warm arms around me and holds tight.

"Have you seen my mom yet? Do you know what's happening?"

I shake my head against his chest, remembering how Ellie looked, being swallowed up by Liz and her parents. I wish I could have rescued her.

"OK," he says. "We'll just wait. OK."

I nod and wipe my eyes with my wrist. I glance at the other people in here with us. The grandfather who took the phone from me is with a woman who must be his wife. She's holding a balloon in the shape of a teddy bear. A younger couple is playing cards and laughing. Some guy is on a cell phone, smiling and saying, "Yeah! Yeah! Can you believe it?"

I hide my face in Caleb's chest. I don't want those happy people to see me. See us. There should be a separate place for people like us. The ones who aren't waiting for happy news. Who aren't waiting to welcome the newest member into our family. Who aren't waiting to find out if it's a boy or girl, or rushing out to smoke a cigar or whatever people do when someone they love has a baby they plan to take home with them. They really should have a special room for people like us.

chapter 35

Ellie

THEY ARE ALL AROUND ME. Taking my clothes off. Wrapping me in a strange-smelling hospital gown with clowns on it. Helping me onto a bed. Pressing against my stomach. Telling me to put my feet in these stirrups and to try to relax.

It will hurt less if I just relax.

How can I relax when I feel like I'm going to die?

My parents hover near me, waiting to be told to leave.

"Who is Liz?" The doctor asks as he goes over my chart and my birth plan.

Liz steps near me and takes my hand. She and my mother exchange a look, and I think I see shame on my mother's face.

My mother steps closer to me. For the first time since I can remember, she puts her hand on my face. "Ellie," she says.

"We'll take good care of her," the doctor says, gently ushering my parents out of the room.

Another contraction starts, and I gasp at the sharpness.

"Try to breathe." The nurse says as she holds my knees apart. I try to squeeze them together. But she's too strong.

"You have to let me do this, hon," she says. "You have to let the doctor see."

The doctor shines a light between my legs. He's not one of the doctors I visited before. I don't know him.

"Please don't!" I cry. "Please stop!"

But his fingers reach inside to feel. The pain is so sharp, I lose my breath.

"No! Nooooooo!"

Liz's hands hold my head. One of her tears drips onto my face and mixes with mine.

"Liz! Make him stop! Please!"

But he keeps pressing and feeling and it hurts so much. Oh, God, it hurts so much.

I squeeze my legs together again.

"Don't," he says sternly. "I know this is uncomfortable, but I have to feel."

"No! Get away from me! I hate you! Liz! Help me!"

He finally moves back and nods at the nurse. The nurse looks at Liz. Liz nods back. There's worry in their eyes.

"The baby is in a breech position," the doctor says to me. "Do you know what that means?"

I've seen illustrations in one of my childbirth books. I nod.

"You'll have to have a C-section."

I nod again.

He gives the nurse more orders I don't understand.

Liz kisses my forehead and holds her tear-soaked cheek against mine. When she moves away, she winks at me, despite that sad face.

The doctor steps closer, and I squeeze my legs together. "I'm going to go give your parents an update, and then we'll get started as soon as the room is ready and the nurses have you prepped, OK?"

I nod again and he leaves.

In the operating room, I close my eyes against the hurt I've been numbed to. Against the nurses standing beside me, trying to smile reassuringly. Against their looks of pity. Against the cloth in front of me so I can't see my belly and what they are about to do. I close my eyes.

I am not here.

I'm going away.

I won't hear their voices. I will not hear them cut me open. I will not feel them reaching for my baby inside me. I will just close my eyes.

Until I hear that sound.

Crying.

My baby is crying.

I have to look.

When I open my eyes, I see his little red body, covered with my blood. Little red fists flailing. Little red feet kicking. Little red face. Little eyes squinched tightly closed. Little open mouth in the shape of an *O*. Screeching.

My hand reaches out, trembling. "Please," I say.

The nurse turns to me with glassy eyes. "Don't worry, hon. We'll bring him back so you can hold him."

But my body hurts with emptiness.

Later, when it's over, after they stitch me back up and bring me to my room, the nurse helps me cradle him in my arms. He stops crying and nestles his face in my neck. I breathe in his sweet smell and fill my lungs with him. My heart.

When he falls asleep, I adjust him so I can memorize his pink and wrinkled face.

"Open your eyes," I whisper.

But he doesn't understand.

Please open your eyes, I say inside my head. *Just once. So you see who I am. So you can see I don't really want to give you away.*

"Are you ready?" the nurse asks.

I study the scrunched face again, then lift him to my own face and press my lips to his soft little forehead. My tears dampen his warm cheek. My heart breaks with the weight of him about to leave my chest.

It's not too late to say I've changed my mind. To keep him after all. And yet I know I won't.

"I'm sorry," I whisper. "I love you."

I close my eyes when the nurse takes him out of my arms. I can't open them again. I can't open them again and see him not here.

When I fall asleep, I dream that I'm chasing after him. But the nurse is carrying him away.

"I changed my mind!" I yell. But she keeps getting farther away.

"I changed my mind! Come back!" But she turns a corner. When I get there and look for her, she's gone.

"I changed my mind," I say to the emptiness. "I changed my mind."

When I wake up, everything hurts. My mother and father are standing over me. They look pale and old.

I don't know what to say to their sad, worried faces. Their disappointed faces.

"Can we get you anything, honey?" my dad asks.

I know he means a glass of water or some more drugs. But I want to tell him to go get my baby back. To go get back the one person who would truly love me. To go get back everything that I lost.

I shake my head.

My mother puts her hand on my forehead the way she did when I was little to check if I had a fever. Her hand is cold on me. I close my eyes until she takes it off.

It's too late for her to touch me now. It's too late for her to be my mother.

She steps back a little.

"The nurses said you can come home soon," my father says. "Maybe the day after tomorrow. They said things look good." Then his shoulders begin to shake, and he starts to cry. He turns away and walks over to the window.

My mother doesn't go to him. She stares across my bed, over me, at his back.

I close my eyes and wait for her to leave. But instead she sinks down onto the chair next to my bed. I listen to her breathe and then start to cry. I keep my eyes shut tightly to lock my own tears inside. But they leak out anyway.

When her hand touches mine, I let it stay there. She rests it lightly on top of mine, then more firmly. Slowly, our hands start to warm each other.

Finally, I turn my palm over and open it to hers. Then I carefully open my eyes and look into her sad face.

The corners of her mouth turn up just slightly, even though she's still crying. This time, she doesn't turn away. She keeps hold of my hand and doesn't let go.

chapter 36

Josh

THERE'S A ROW OF BABIES in clear plastic bed things lined up to face the window. They look strange, all wrapped up like mummies so you can't see their arms or legs, and those little caps so all you can see is their squishy faces.

I stand here staring at them, thinking eventually one of them will open their eyes. And I'll know. Somehow I'll know that's the one.

The nurses give me looks from the other side of the glass. They must think I'm a big brother, or an uncle or something. They smile at me, as if to say, *How sweet, a boy his age looking at babies.*

I turn away from them.

A man and woman come out of a room holding hands. The woman's wearing a bathrobe and still looks like she's pregnant. The man helps her hobble over to the window next to me and they peer in.

"Isn't she beautiful?" the woman asks.

The man puts his arm around her and pulls her to him. "Just like her mom."

I watch their reflections in the glass. The woman's hair is all over the place like she just woke up. The man needs a shave. I try to figure out which baby they're looking at, but they all look the same.

"I never thought—" the man starts to say, but he gets all choked up and starts to cry.

The woman laughs. "You'd be so emotional?"

He laughs, too. "Something like that."

They stare quietly after that. Being the perfect parents. Not noticing me.

"Let's have the nurse bring her back to the room," the wife says.

"You need your rest, honey," the husband answers.

She rests her head on his shoulder. "I know. But it's so hard to leave her."

I study the babies and notice the small labels at the foot of their little beds that list their names. I try to read the names on the tags, but they're hard to make out. Baby Finnegan. Baby Hirokane. Baby Jacobson. I don't see Ellie's last name. Maybe they wouldn't even use it. The bed on the end is turned in a way so you can't see the name from the window. Maybe they don't want anyone to see. Maybe this could be the one. I knew my chances of seeing the baby were pretty slim. I figured the adoptive parents would take the baby right away and disappear to their happy anonymous home. But maybe I had it wrong. I could have everything wrong.

My heart pounds in my chest as I walk around the man and woman to get closer. The baby is sound asleep. Somehow it managed to get a hand out of the tight-fitting blanket, and its tiny fist hangs out. Even though the baby's asleep, that tight little fist makes it look angry.

Without realizing, I've made fists with my own hands. I look down at them, then back at the baby's.

A nurse walks over to the baby and checks something from a file attached to the end of the plastic bed. She tucks the hand back into the blanket, gently pats the baby's head, then moves on to the next one.

But her touch wakes the baby up and the little fist escapes

again. I tap gently on the glass. The nurse looks up at me, as if I was trying to get her attention. *Not you*, I want to say. But I pull my hand away from the glass. The baby doesn't see me.

"It'll be a while before he learns to wave," the man says to me, like I'm an idiot. "He can't even see beyond a few inches now."

I don't say anything back. I just look at the baby again.

I guess the guy's right. It must be a boy, since the little cap on his head is blue.

"C'mon, honey. You should be resting." The man guides the woman away.

I stand alone, staring at the baby's crinkled face, his tiny, angry fist. He closes his eyes again, and his hand seems to relax a little. I flatten my own hand against the glass.

Good-bye, baby. Good luck.

I turn and slowly walk down the long hallway, past the waiting room filled with excited relatives, past the admissions desk, past the lobby where I sat for hours before I got the courage to try and see, and into the hot afternoon sun.

I walk all the way home. All three miles. I walk and think about that tiny, bundled-up baby I'll never know. I think about that face as long as I can so I won't forget it.

When I reach the driveway, I hear music coming from the house. It's my dad practicing. He thinks I'm still at Caleb's. I walk up the driveway slowly. Listening. He's not so much singing but humming. The sound is vaguely familiar. Like a lullaby.

I stand in the doorway and keep listening. Rosie sits in front of him while he plays. He messes up a few times, but he keeps going. When he finishes, Rosie notices me standing in the doorway and comes over to lick my hand.

My dad jumps when he sees me and looks embarrassed. He puts the guitar next to him on the couch and nods at me.

"I used to play that for you when you were little. Remember? It was the only way your mom and I could get you to go to sleep."

"Yeah," I lie. I wish I could remember. I wish I could remember him singing to me. Loving me. I wonder how often he sits here alone, playing these old lullabies to the dog.

My dad sighs, and Rosie jogs back over to him and puts her head in his lap.

I stay in the doorway. After walking so long in the bright sunlight, I feel like I'm stepping into a dark cave.

"You OK, bud?"

I nod. The sun shines hot on my back.

Only a few seconds go by, but it seems like longer.

My dad and Rosie both wait, watching me.

But I can't go in there.

"You sure you're all right, son?" my dad asks. He stands up. Rosie wags her tail.

The sun beats down on my shoulders as I take a step back.

"Yeah," I tell him. "I just—need to take a walk."

My dad takes a step toward me. "You want company?"

My throat tightens. I swallow to keep myself together.

"Nah," I say, only it sort of sounds like a croak. "You should stay and keep playing. It sounds—nice."

When our eyes meet, I feel my heart start to crack.

"Really," I say.

I push the door closed and nod at him through the screen. "Thanks for the offer, though," I manage.

I start down the driveway, not sure where to go.

The truth is, I feel like I could walk forever. Like I could walk down to the end of the driveway and keep going.

Too bad there's nowhere for me to end up but right back here.

I walk anyway. Just walk and walk. Past all the things I know. All these ugly parts of town. When I get near my dad's garage, I don't want to look at it, but I have to. At the grease-stained pavement and the cracked window patched with duct tape so it crosses out the black-and-orange cardboard OPEN sign hanging inside, making it read O EN. At the long row of cars and trucks waiting to be fixed and tuned and detailed and set free. At the Coke machine flickering in the sun with half its choices showing EMPTY.

I turn away from it all and keep walking. Faster. I'm like one of those crazy speed walkers, only I'm not swinging my arms back and forth. Cars whiz by me. I smell their exhaust and the hot tar from the road. I walk all the way back to town again.

My feet are sweaty and slippery inside my sneakers. My shirt is wet against my back. My face prickles with sweat.

I keep my pace, though. All the way to the nursing home. I only slow down when I get to the entrance. I haven't been here since my mom first got the job and dragged me over for a tour and to meet all her nosy co-workers, who, of course, asked why she hadn't brought Hal along, even though I'm sure they knew the answer, those bastards.

I push the handicapped button and the door swings open. I don't know why I'm suddenly so pissed off. But I walk straight up to the reception desk and—and stall. What the hell am I doing here?

"Can I help you?" A youngish-looking guy behind the desk looks at me curiously. I'm sure I look like a raging psycho by now and, to be honest, I feel like one.

"I need to see my mother," I say.

He raises his eyebrows. "Her name?"

"Uh, Jennifer. Jennifer Sawyer."

"One minute." He picks up the phone and turns away from me. I wipe the sweat off my forehead with the back of my hand.

"She'll be right down."

A few minutes later, the elevator on the far wall dings and the door opens. My mom rushes out. My eyes start to well up as soon as I see her.

"Josh?" She rushes toward me. "Are you OK?"

All the breath comes out of me. I start to sag. She takes hold of my arm.

"Honey?"

"I need to talk to you."

She leads me outside to an empty group of picnic tables and sits me down. She sits across from me but right away reaches over for my hands and looks at me with worried eyes.

"What is it, honey? Tell me what's the matter."

"It's over," I say, squeezing her hands harder, even though mine are sweaty and gross.

"Oh, Josh," she says.

"I—I went to try to see him," I say. "I think I saw my baby, and—" But I can't say anything else because I'm sobbing big, heaving sobs. I can't tell her that I think I might go crazy not knowing if that baby behind the glass was mine. My mom lets go of my hands and comes around to my side of the table and holds me. She hugs me tight while I cry it all out of me. Until I'm empty.

When I can speak, I tell her about the night I talked with my dad. How I know I was a mistake. I tell her I don't understand why she can't be near us anymore. How sometimes I wish I could disappear, or that I'd never been born. I tell her how Ellie and I were only together once and that I tried to do everything right but I did everything wrong. That I didn't mean to hurt her. But I'd ruined her life. And I wasn't sure I could live knowing that.

And all the time I tell her these things, she just listens and holds me like she did when I was little. She looks off at the trees on the other side of the table and runs her fingers over the top of my head in this soothing way she used to do when I was a kid and had a fever and couldn't sleep.

"I'm here now," she tells me in a quiet voice. "I'm here. I'm going to help you get through this, Joshy. I promise."

I let her hold me. I squeeze my eyes shut and let her hang on as long as she can. But as hard as I want to believe her, I don't think she can really help me. No more than I can help her.

chapter 37

Caleb

WHEN MY MOM CAME to tell us it was over and that Ellie was OK, I just stood there. I don't know what I expected, but I didn't feel relieved. I just felt sad.

Corinne wobbled a little next to me as my mom gave us the details. Ellie was fine. The procedure went well. The baby was a healthy boy. As I stood next to Corinne, I could feel her unravel. I reached for her small hand. She pressed her thin arm against mine, and I held her up. After my mom left to go back and check on Ellie, we walked outside into the bright sun and found a bench to sit on. Corinne started crying. I wrapped my arms around her and let her cry into my chest while she told me what an awful friend she thought she'd been. I tried to tell her she was wrong, but she just shook her head. The whole time, I kept thinking about Josh and how I felt like I'd let him down, too. How I hadn't done enough to see things from his point of view. I should have talked to him more and told him I understood. I should have driven him to the hospital or asked Ellie if he could see the baby since I know Josh would never ask himself. I should have helped him find out what his rights were, so he could see the baby, maybe even hold him if he wanted to. But I didn't. And he cared too much about not hurting Ellie any more than he already had, to ask.

Now Corinne and I are waiting at the hospital again. Just like yesterday and the day before. Waiting for the doctors to let Ellie go home. For everything to be final.

Each day Corinne and I sit here, holding hands but not looking at each other. I wait while Corinne goes to see Ellie. Each time she comes back, she looks the same. Sad and empty. Worried. She leans her head on my shoulder and stares at our hands. I can't be sure, but I think, on top of everything else, Corinne is wondering the same thing I am. What will happen to *us*?

Now I squeeze her hand without thinking and she rubs her thumb along mine. She's watching a little girl sitting on the rug. I wonder if she even realizes she's responding to me.

I lean my head back against the couch just as my mom walks into the room, wringing her hands.

"Ellie's parents are taking her home in a few hours," she says. "Everything's been — finalized." She seems to choke on the word. "I'll see you back at the house later and we'll talk." She hurries off and leaves us standing there, Corinne's warm hand in mine, both of us unsure of what to do next.

Neither of us moves.

Finally, Corinne gently pulls me up off the couch and out of the room. I let her lead me outside to her car.

We drive past the park. Past our merry-go-round. And the seesaw. And the swings. Past the road to Ellie's house. Past Josh's.

When we get to my house, Corinne leads me upstairs. Somehow she knows where my bedroom is even though she's never been here. She pulls back my comforter and guides me onto the bed and lies down next to me. I stretch out my arm and she rolls closer to me so the side of her face rests on my chest. I can feel my heart beat against her cheek.

When we wake up, the house is quiet.

Corinne sits up. "We fell asleep," she says.

"What time is it?"

She reaches for my alarm clock. "After five." She falls back into the pillow and pushes in closer to me and I get my arms around her. Her tiny body feels so good and safe. I want to stay like this forever.

"Are you OK?" she asks. She lifts her face to mine, and I kiss her forehead.

"Yeah. Are you?"

She nods and kisses my chin.

And then we kiss on the lips. Softly at first, then deeply. I can barely breathe.

Corinne reaches her hand under my shirt. It sends prickles of heat through my body. I get hard against her leg and immediately feel like an asshole because I didn't mean for this to happen. But she feels so good and I've been dying for this moment for weeks. Only it doesn't feel right. Not now.

She pulls back. "I'm sorry," she says. "I didn't mean for us to—"

"Me either." I roll away a little.

"I mean I want to—just—not right now."

"Me, too," I say.

We lie next to each other, both staring at the ceiling. The heat slowly drains out of me.

"I'm sorry," I finally say.

She doesn't answer. The floor creaks downstairs. I wonder if my mom's home, and if she knows we're up here, in my bed. At the same time, I realize I don't really care.

"Corinne?" I turn to face her profile and see a tear slowly make its way across her temple and onto my pillow.

I trace the trail and wipe it clear with my thumb.

She turns to face me and smiles as another tear follows the same path.

"I love you," I say.

She moves closer to me, turning her head again so her head tucks into my neck and we feel like a finished puzzle.

"I love you, too," she whispers.

chapter 38

Corinne

MY FAVORITE PART OF THE LAST WEEK of school used to be cleaning out my locker and leaving it empty behind me. Shutting the door for the last time, hard, and hearing that echo inside.

But today *I* feel empty. Even before I close my locker door.

I got here early on purpose, before anyone else is around and the halls become a sea of balled-up paper and used spiral notebooks and people pushing and shoving to get out.

I quickly make my way down the quiet hallway to Ellie's locker. I told her I'd get her stuff for her and return her books. Before I open the door, I look at the word there. Scratched and mean. I never understood exactly why Ellie didn't cover it up, but I think maybe she felt like she deserved it.

It must have been horrible to walk to her locker every day, seeing that word and feeling it was true. I know it's only a word. Sticks and stones and all that crap. Right. Whoever made up that stupid saying was totally high.

I reach into my pocket and pull out a piece of paper with Ellie's locker combination on it. I turn the dial until the lock clicks open.

There isn't much inside, just a few notebooks and some decorations. There's the heart magnet I gave her in the seventh grade holding up her schedule, and a worn-looking plaid shirt hanging on the coat hook. It's the one we got at the Salvation Army. I pull it out and touch the soft fabric. It smells like Ellie. I know she probably won't want it back, but I tie it around my waist anyway. Then I put the rest of her stuff in my backpack and close the door.

The word glares at me.

I know what I have to do. I've been planning this ever since Caleb and I were in the waiting room at the hospital.

There was a little girl in the room with us, sitting on the floor. She and her father were waiting for her baby brother or sister to be born. She had a notebook she was writing in, and I managed to get a quick peek. She'd written the word *MOTHER* down the margin and then started writing words that began with each letter. But they weren't nice words, like "marvelous" or "terrific." Instead she'd written, *Mean* for *M*, *Ogre* for *O*, *Terrible* for *T*. That was as far as she'd gotten. I did the same thing with Ava when I was little. We'd pick a dirty word and think of more dirty words that began with each letter. My sister had a great vocabulary even then.

I search through my bag and find the red metallic marker I bought at the craft store. When I take off the cap, the smell reminds me of nail polish and Saturday mornings when Ellie still spent the night at my house. We'd get up late and paint our toenails while we watched cartoons. We never do that anymore.

I look around to make sure the hallway is still empty before I start to write. The letters are thick and red and bright. I blow on them until the shiny ink dries, then step back.

*S*he is my best friend

*L*isten

U didn't know her

*T*oo bad

The words look kind of odd, going up instead of across, but I think Ellie would like it. I think she would laugh, watching people try to read my words, their heads tilted to one side. She'll probably never see them, though. Over the summer they'll give the lockers and walls a new coat of paint so we can all start fresh in the fall. But there's still today. And Ellie wasn't here to tell me not to.

I swing my backpack over my shoulder and walk down the hall without looking back. I leave those words behind me, red and almost happy-seeming, and I laugh just a little. For Ellie.

chapter 39

Caleb

CORINNE, MY MOM, AND ELLIE are sitting in the old Adirondack chairs on the back lawn. I watch them from my bedroom window. They sit in the shade, their shoes kicked off, legs crossed, bare feet swinging in the air. They're drinking lemonade in clear glasses. Once in a while they laugh about something. The sound makes it seem like things really are going to be OK.

My mom's big, floppy hat bops around while she rants about something. Corinne shoves her shoulder gently, and they all crack up again.

I take the stairs two at a time and stroll outside, trying not to look too eager to join them.

"Here's our boy!" my mom calls. "Come sit with us!"

Corinne turns and waves me forward. As I walk across the warm grass, I see her coy grin under her hat. It's one of my mom's straw ones and looks ridiculous in a cute way. I want to grab her hand and race up to my room with her. I can tell by the way she looks at me that she'd like that, too.

Lately being alone together is what we live for. We sit around waiting for my mom to go shopping or to her art class. As soon as her car turns out of the driveway we race up the stairs. Corinne says we have to make up for all those months we stayed away from each other. I think it's more about all those months we were so worried and scared of what was going to happen with Ellie and Josh. And now that it's over, it's about us. Together. Being happy without feeling guilty.

Corinne gives me a sly look. She winks at me before she leans back in her chair and closes her eyes to let the sun warm her face.

I sit on the grass near their feet. Even though this setup is familiar—me sitting below them like this—I don't feel like an outsider anymore. I don't feel guilty for being a guy.

I reach for my mom's glass and take a sip.

"Ew, boy germs," Corinne says. "You're going to let him share your glass?" She winks at me.

I take a long swig. It's sweet and sour and ice cold.

My mom leans forward and squeezes my shoulders.

Ellie smiles at me and then looks off toward the quiet road. Her right hand rests on her stomach. I can't imagine the emptiness she must feel. I wish there was something we could do for her, but my mom says just hanging out with her like this will help. Just trying to be normal, whatever that means.

I stay for a while, letting my mom and Corinne tease me while I finish off my mom's drink. Then I stand up and take their empty glasses as an excuse to go back inside and leave them alone. I put the glasses in the sink and look out the window at them.

There are so many things I want to know. Like if Ellie knows where the baby is or who the new parents are. But I'll never ask. I'll just have to wonder, and hope he has a good life.

Josh doesn't talk to me about the baby. He says he can't yet. But he knows he can come to me when he needs to, and I think that helps a little. He wrote a letter to Ellie, apologizing for what happened. He made me read it first to make sure it was OK. It was perfect.

I walk into the living room and stand in front of my dad's portrait. My mom calls it her masterpiece. I study my father's distant expression. I used to hate him for abandoning me. For not caring. But I realize now I don't need him. I never needed him. I have my mom, and Corinne. I even have Josh. And that's enough. It's plenty.

chapter 40

Josh

THE HOUSE IS QUIET AND DARK. Rosie is doing her nightly guard duty, sleeping in the hall between the door to my room and the one to my parents'. She lifts her head when I step into the hallway. I reach down and give her a pat. She thumps her tail and lets me go.

Outside, it's just the right amount of darkness, when the sun is completely gone and won't be back for a few hours at least. I move silently down the driveway like a cat.

The first time I did this I stumbled all over the place. The streetlights don't really do much, so it's hard to find your way. But I've been doing this every night for three weeks, and I could probably walk with my eyes closed. I've been biding my time till I move in with my uncle and start senior year at a new school where no one knows me. Someplace Ellie won't have to see me every day. And I guess so I won't have to see her.

Caleb and Dave were pretty upset when I told them, but they'll get over it. They understand. My parents say a fresh start is probably a good idea, but they both look sad when they say it. I wish it meant a fresh start for them, too. But who am I kidding? Is there really such a thing? Whatever. One more month and I'll be out of here.

The crickets and frogs sing away as I walk through the warm, dark air, all the way to the chain-link fence. I run my hands along it until I come to the gate. Then I stop. I put my fingers through the metal wires and push. The gate whines as I move it forward.

I walk across the dew-covered grass, cut smooth by the same ancient guy who's been cutting it every summer since I was a kid. Dave, Caleb, and I used to beg him to give us a ride on his mower. He never did. He always said he would if he could, but it might get him fired. Or that if he gave us a ride, then he'd have to give all the other kids one. But he knew we were the only ones around. We were the only ones that came every day, by ourselves. We were the only ones who really needed a ride on that stupid mower with him.

When I get to the swings, hanging still in the darkness, I'm almost afraid to touch them. Just like always.

I know her hands touched these chains. She sat on this seat, with the baby inside her. Swinging inside her. And so this is all I have left.

The last day of school I went to her locker to fix the word, but someone already had. Probably Corinne. I couldn't even do that for Ellie.

I screwed up even that.

I turn around and reach for the chains, back up with my legs, and let go.

I start pumping.

The warm air blows against my face.

I close my eyes.

I fly forward, then fall back.

I pump harder, rising higher with each swing.

But it's always the same.

No matter how far I go forward, I swing back just as hard and fast.

I keep trying anyway.

I keep thinking, maybe this will be the night.

Maybe I don't have to wait another month.

Maybe this time,

if I pump hard enough,

I can jump off

and fly

right

out

of

here.

chapter 41
Ellie

CORINNE IS DRAGGING ME to the grocery store. She wants to buy cake mix for Caleb's birthday party. She thinks it will cheer me up to bake a cake. I don't tell her about the dream I had last night. The same dream I have almost every night.

I'm in the hospital, holding him. He's all wrinkled and red, the way he was when he was born. So small and fragile-looking. At first I'm afraid I'll hurt him. He's so little. But as my arms get used to him, I relax. I lean forward and kiss his soft little head. His dark eyes look into mine. He's such a warm little bundle in my arms. Even though he's tiny, I feel his solid weight against me. Until a nurse comes and lifts him out of my arms. And I wake up cold and weightless.

"Where's the damn baking aisle?"

Corinne doesn't see me touch my empty stomach. She doesn't know I trace the scar with my finger before I fall asleep. Most people don't even know I have the scar. People who don't know me don't stare at me anymore. They don't give me those disapproving looks. They can't tell by looking at me, the things that I've done. They can't tell I ever had a baby. Or that I gave him away.

I'm following Corinne down the cereal aisle when I see him. The baby boy. He looks right at me and smiles. I glance around to see who's watching. The woman pushing his cart is a few feet away, comparing labels on Cheerios and Special K boxes.

She doesn't see me smile back at him. She doesn't see him reach toward me with his tiny hand, like he wants me to pick him up and carry him away.

I step closer, ready to take him. Ready to lift him out of that seat and run. But then Corinne is behind me with three cans of frosting and I have to help her decide which one Caleb would like best.

Before we go, I turn toward him again. Corinne turns, too. He sticks out his hand and reaches.

"Bye-bye," Corinne says. "Look how cute, Ellie. He's waving bye-bye."

Corinne waves back. She doesn't understand that he's too

little to know how to wave. Only I know he's reaching for something. For his mother. For me?

I start to go back to him. But then the woman is there. He makes a giggly noise when he sees her. She kisses him on the nose.

Corinne takes my hand. "C'mon, El. Let's go." Her hand is warm and strong in mine.

I squeeze it, and she squeezes back. I start to say OK, but the word gets caught in my throat. So I just nod.

Corinne pulls me down the aisle, away from the baby. Past Tony the Tiger and Fruity Pebbles and the Lucky Charms leprechaun.

I don't turn around, but I can still hear him behind us.

"Gaaaaaaaaaaa," he cries just before we turn the corner.

Good-bye.

Acknowledgments

Many thanks are owed to all the people who've read this novel at various stages, and there have been several. Thank you to early readers Lowry Pei, Marguerite W. Davol, Sarah Aronson, Michelle D. Kwasney, Kevin Slattery, Diane Raymond, Patricia and Louis Carini, and everyone in my Hatfield Writers' Group. Thank you to Cecil Castellucci for believing in me, cheering me on, and saying just the right words to keep me going. Thanks to my WWaWWa sisters, Cindy Faughnan and Debbi Michiko Florence, who read multiple drafts, and who always, *always*, are there when I need them. Someday, ladies, we really will go to Tuscany. To my agent, Barry Goldblatt, for not giving up on *The Novel Formerly Known as Slut*. To my kind and generous editor, Joan Powers, who never fails to help me find the way. Extra special thanks to my husband, Peter Carini, as always, for everything. And finally, thank you to the Society of Children's Book Writers and Illustrators for awarding me the Work-in-Progress Grant for a Contemporary Novel, which provided funding for child care for my then two-year-old son, which in turn provided me with the time to complete the very first draft.